Caught in the Storm

Read/Write: POWER, not skill.
Logical/analytical

Sibiri's initiation rite is akin to giving birth

Caught in the
Storm

Seydou Badian

Translated by
Marie-Thérèse Noiset

A THREE CONTINENTS BOOK
LYNNE RIENNER PUBLISHERS
BOULDER & LONDON

Published in the United States of America in 1998 by
Lynne Rienner Publishers, Inc.
1800 30th Street, Boulder, Colorado 80301

and in the United Kingdom by
Lynne Rienner Publishers, Inc.
3 Henrietta Street, Covent Garden, London WC2E 8LU

Translated from *Sous l'orage* with the permission of La Société
Nouvelle Présence Africaine

Library of Congress Cataloging-in-Publication Data
Badian, Seydou, 1928–
  [Sous l'orage (Kany). English]
  Caught in the storm / by Seydou Badian ; translated by
  Marie-Thérèse Noiset.
    p. cm.
  ISBN 0-89410-793-3 (cloth). — ISBN 0-89410-794-1 (paper)
  I. Title.
PQ3989.2.K6S613 1998
843—dc20
                                                    95-51197
                                                       CIP
                                                        AC

British Cataloguing in Publication Data
A Cataloguing in Publication record for this book
is available from the British Library

Printed and bound in the United States of America

    The paper used in this publication meets the requirements
⊗ of the American National Standard for Permanence of
    Paper for Printed Library Materials Z39.48-1984.

  5 4 3 2 1

Introduction

Marie-Thérèse Noiset

In his preface to the 1963 edition of *Caught in the Storm*, Charles Camproux underscores the gentle tone of the novel. He attributes it to Africa's and, in particular, to Seydou Badian's sense of humanity. He praises Badian for reaching beyond materialistic considerations in order "to understand those who long to be understood, to love those who long to be loved." And indeed, Badian allows a diversity of voices to be heard; but in spite of its warm tone, this novel offers much more than an idealistic approach to the colonial situation. It gives a true exegesis of African culture and a complete revaluation of the situation at hand by enlightened African wisdom.

Caught in the Storm was written in 1954, a time when Africa was reassessing itself, as the title of the novel implies. The French, convinced of the superiority of their culture, had tried to impose their ways on their West African colonies since the end of the nineteenth century. They built schools to educate the brightest children and even sent some of them to study in France. But from the 1930s, an African elite emerged that began to defend the value of their own civilization and to take a strong interest in politics. Badian belongs to the second generation of this intellectual group. Born in Bamako, Mali (then French Sudan), in 1928, he received his elementary education in his native city. He was then sent to secondary school in Montpellier, where he later enrolled in the faculty of medicine at the university and became a medical doctor in 1955. When he wrote *Caught in the Storm*, Badian had not yet engaged in the political activities that brought him both fame and trouble in his country. In 1957 he became minister of rural economy and planning of Sudan. In 1960, he held the same position in Mali, under the rule of Modibo Keita, and in 1962, he was made minister of development. He was a leader of the radical Marxist group in Keita's government. His political essay "Les dirigeants africains face à leur peuple," which won the *Grand Prix Littéraire de l'Afrique Noire,* was published in 1964. Badian was arrested when Keita's regime was overthrown in 1968 and was imprisoned for ten years.

Although still young when he wrote *Caught in the Storm,* Badian had already been exposed to many streams of thought, and the novel expresses many of his political, economic, and social concerns. It brilliantly demonstrates that the French policy of *assimilation,* trying to substitute French culture for the one in place, had been totally wrong. Wiser than their French rulers, the characters in *Caught in the Storm* end up understanding and accepting the value of different cultures.

Caught in the Storm confronts the problems of Africa in a very subtle way. Many of its characters are ideological opposites, but they share a common *Négritude,* and this is what brings them back together in the end. The common bond reconciles traditional and modern ways of thinking and bridges the gap between generations.

Négritude has been a controversial concept over the years. It has been praised to the skies, suspected of being racist, and accused of extreme conservativism. But it has also, since the term was coined by Césaire in *Cahier d'un retour au pays natal* in 1939, allowed Africans to recapture their very identity from European encroachment. Abiola Irele defines Senghor's *Négritude*:

> For him *Négritude* is an inner state of the black man, and lies outside the historical process. It is first and foremost a distinctive mode of being and of existence, particular to the black man, which can be deduced from his way of life—and which constitutes his *identity*, in the original sense of the word. (*The African Experience in Literature and Ideology*, pp. 69–70)

This is also the *Négritude* found in Badian's novel. It is a way of being, a quality inherent to the person. It does not render life impervious to change, but it processes change in a fashion that no amount of European influence can eradicate.

It is worth noting that Badian's novel, which was first published as *Kany*, was later renamed *Caught in the Storm*. On first impression, Kany may indeed be perceived as the heroine of the book. The entire story centers on her impending marriage: will she, the sweet, young, educated maiden, be allowed to marry Samou, her high school sweetheart, or will she have to obey her father's orders and become the third wife of Famagan, the merchant? Actually Kany herself can do very little to shape her future. Like her mother, she can only hope and pray that decisions will be made in her favor. It is among men that resolutions are made in this strongly paternalistic society. Badian uses Kany as a pawn on the chessboard to show Black Africa wisely working its way out of the turmoil brought about by European rule.

Kany's family is presented as deeply divided in spite of its surface unity: her father, Old Benfa, and Sibiri, his eldest son, are the keepers of traditional values and customs. Her younger brothers, Birama, Nianson, and Karamoko, who are school educated, welcome with

enthusiasm the scientific trends and the general modern-
ism of Europe.

These differences may seem irreconcilable, but once
they are stated, Badian does not harp on them. Instead,
he makes a case for Africa. Traditional life is presented in
a way that elicits awe and deep respect. Starting with the
recounting of Sibiri's initiation rites, it is the solidarity of
the African spirit that is stressed:

> I am nothing without him.
> If he slips and stumbles,
> I stumble with him if I cannot keep from falling. (p. 11)

So sing the young men of their fellow initiates on the
threshold of manhood. They perceive each individual, living or dead, as a useful and necessary link in the human
chain. They bestow praise and admiration on the wisdom
and accomplishments of their elders and ancestors:

> They have preceded me in everything,
> I will receive from their hands
> That wisdom that I will in turn hand on
> To those who will follow me. (p. 11)

This philosophy, while ensuring a smooth but un-
changeable continuity, puts an enormous burden of responsibility on the individual. It requires sharp awareness
and total social commitment. When it is time for Kany to
marry, her father must assume responsibility for the choice
of a husband and make sure that the marriage suits the
family. He consults with his brothers, but they in turn
place their entire trust in his wisdom because he is the
eldest.

The young, for their part, do not take a radical stand
against traditional life. Birama, Kany's younger brother,
and Sidi, Samou's best friend, speak up for the rights of
women, but they do not otherwise go against tradition. As

for Kany and Samou, while they fervently hope that their love will prevail, they do not criticize the African system. From the start, Samou proves to be an enlightened young man able to appreciate his own culture and to sort out the good and the bad that Europe has brought to his people.

Faced with the problem of making his daughter accept the husband that has been chosen for her, Benfa sends Kany and Birama on a trip to the remote village of Old Djigui, his hunter brother. He hopes that Djigui will help him convince the young people of the rightness of African tradition. The trip opens the way to discussions of an economic and political nature. Various people on the train and in the village express their discontent with the whites and suggest a readiness to take over the economic and political leadership of the country.

The stay in the village serves yet another significant purpose. It exposes Kany and Birama to a kind of life that they had not had a chance to experience in the city: life untouched by European influence. They first react with fear and disgust to the discomforts and archaic practices they encounter, but Old Djigui transforms their initial shock into a longing to learn more about village life. Feeling that his niece and nephew have been cheated by their bookish education, he sets out to acquaint them with the ancestral values of restraint, courage, and solidarity. The two young people are fascinated by Djigui's knowledge of the wild as well as by his committed philosophy of life. "Man," he tells the young city dwellers, "is a little like a tall tree: every traveler has a right to his shade" (p. 70).

As the annual feast of the hunters approaches, Birama feels more and more drawn toward his people and the mysterious events that are to take place. He asks to be allowed to participate in the formal ceremonies, but Old Djigui rejects his request because he has been raised among white people. However, after considerable soul searching, the old man, who has grown to love Birama, rationalizes that a stay among Europeans cannot change a person's inner nature. Preparing to appear at the formal night gathering of the hunters with his nephew at his side, Old Djigui proudly says to himself: "I will tell them [his hunting companions]: he has been with the white men for seven years, and now he has come back to us." And jubilant, he goes on: "And I will add: soaking in water never turned a tree trunk into a crocodile" (p. 74).

To strengthen Djigui's vibrant hymn to *Négritude*, Badian deftly introduces a new character into his story. He is Tiéman, the healer, who when faced with the necessity of making a choice between the European and African ways of life, opted for Africa. School educated and only a few steps away from being a teacher, Tiéman chose to become a healer in his native village. He never tries to convince anyone of the correctness of his decision; he merely explains how he arrived at it. One evening, when he was a soldier in Europe, he and some of his friends were requested to furnish the entertainment for the evening—they were asked to present African dances to their European friends. Only the few who had never been to school were able to do it. This little incident made him realize how important, unique, and fragile ethnic identity was: "That evening made me understand the truth. Mankind would be truly poor if we all turned into Europeans" (p. 88).

Yet, Tiéman recognizes the good points of European culture. He believes that Kany has a right to her own happiness and tries to persuade Old Djigui to talk to his brother on her behalf. He also sees the advantages of modern techniques, but he refuses to lose the ancient moral values to the process of modernization. "Man is not just the one who creates," he writes to Samou, "he is also the one who takes part in the building of the family of man" (p. 90).

Meanwhile, things are stirring in the city. The winds of change are blowing. People begin to envision a new life free from the European grip. A boundless enthusiasm reigns, especially among the young. Progress and technology will be part of their world, but it will be done the African way. They will discuss things among themselves, decide on their own what is best for Africa, and forge ahead together. Samou, the rational, learned young man, sees hope for his country and his future with Kany.

Upon Kany's and Birama's return to the city, Tiéman's advice seems to have been well received. Samou is now welcome by Kany's parents, but this pleasant state of affairs does not last. To their consternation, the young people realize that Old Benfa was just temporizing. True, things are changing, but Old Benfa has promised his daughter to Famagan. How can he go back on his word?

It takes the delicate intervention of Kerfa-the-fool to turn the situation around. Like the fool of ancient times, Kerfa possesses a profound wisdom. A young man, he is considered odd by his peers because he enjoys the company of his elders and understands them. But he is a wise mediator who assumes, in the city, the role that Tiéman played in the village. He takes the cause of Samou and Kany to heart, but he disavows force as a means to problem-solving, and he pleads with the young for comprehension:

> The old people are all confused, and you, you have disappointed them, because what they expected of you was a sympathetic understanding and a gradual, enlightened introduction to the system that is being forced upon them. (p. 107)

At the end of the story, peace is restored because African values have prevailed. The problems have not entirely disappeared, but conciliation and understanding are at work again. Young and old have recaptured the true essence of African life in spite of their differences, and there is hope for the future. The words of Benfa's friend Old Aladji sum up the situation in style, stressing African solidarity and continuity. His confidence renewed, he says of the young:

> Their way, they will find it after having walked paths strewn with thorns, but they will find it, because "from the roots to the leaves, sap rises and never stops." (p. 113)

On that day, Old Benfa had got up earlier than usual. He was up before the first light of dawn. In the courtyard, nothing moved; the only sound heard was the occasional rustling of the leaves of the little mango tree not far from the well. Was it the wind? Or nightbirds? It was hard to tell.

Old Benfa sat down on the little *tara*[1] where, during the day, Mama Téné kept the gourds she used as pots. The *tara* was wet, but the master of the house did not pay much attention to that; he was so worried.... All night long he had tossed and turned on his mat without being able to sleep. How could he have slept with the plans he had in his head? It would have been impossible. Old Benfa pictured himself as being the most important man in the neighborhood for at least a week. The day was not far when the most popular, the most sought after of the bards would sing his praises. He would be the center of attention; people would talk about him. His forefathers, his brothers, and all his relatives would be acclaimed.

What can one do to impress all these people? What can one do to please them? Every detail has to be worked out most carefully so that no one can find fault with anything. Then, how memorable these days will be!!! Bards will recall them in other places, old people will recount

---

1. A *tara* is a raised bed made of puddled clay.

1

them to their grandchildren, and anywhere that Benfa appears people will say with respect and admiration: "That's him!"

Dreaming on the damp *tara*, Kany's father seemed to be tirelessly scanning the horizon. One would have thought that he had important matters to discuss with the sun, which he sought above the dense tops of the *kaïlcedrats*.[2] But the sun had not appeared yet.

Old Benfa got up. He gave the horizon a lingering, melancholy look, and uttering a sigh, pulled out his prayer beads. He took a few steps towards the kitchen, bent down to set straight a fallen gourd, and paused for a moment.

Several times he walked back and forth between the kitchen and the door of the veranda, the silence broken only by the regular click of his prayer beads.

Little by little the sun came out. It nibbled away at the horizon. But in several places it seemed so shy as to hide behind the giant *kaïlcedrats* in the distance. A faint light came over the courtyard. The first birds appeared; life was gradually stirring around the lone figure of Benfa.

With a kick, he knocked down the board that served as a door to the henhouse. He went to the end of the courtyard where he leaned for a moment against the guava tree under which his sheep was grazing. He patted the head and the back of the animal which came and rubbed against him, bleating and sniffing.

Old Benfa was proud of his sheep. The elders of the neighborhood admired him; he was clean and well fed. He often accompanied his master in the street, following him very closely. Old Benfa patted him possessively; he became enraged when children played with the little bell the sheep wore around his neck.

---

2. African trees.

On several occasions merchants had offered considerable sums to Old Benfa, but he would not part with his sheep at any price because his plumpness was proof of the high-quality food that the family enjoyed.

Old Benfa showed off his sheep to everyone who came by: "I bought him only six months ago and he was as skinny as a doe. Look at him now; in a year he won't be able to get through the door."

That sheep was so spoiled by his master that none of his wives dared to complain when the animal ate their millet flour or pieces of their manioc roots.

Old Benfa grumbled and went back to the *tara*. He became even more engrossed in his thoughts.

It was broad daylight now. Mayflies were rising from the damp ground, attracting the birds with their awkward, hesitant flight. From high up in the mango trees, the millet-eaters and a few turtle-doves dashed after this easy prey. They skimmed the ground and flew back to the trees in the midst of the twitterings and flutterings of wings.

Time and again in the sky, storks flew by in V-formation, wild ducks passed, guided by a leader, and dolens spread out their large silvery grey wings with graceful nonchalance.

The hawk was wheeling and the hens answered each of his cries with frightened clucks. Even higher up, the vultures seemed to salute each other with the tips of their wings.

Patiently telling his beads, Old Benfa uttered an invocation in a low voice, ran his two hands over his face three times and turned towards the East. All of a sudden he made a quick gesture as if he was slapping some impertinent kid. It was the little monkey again who, having surreptitiously come up to him, had snatched away his beads.

Boubouny, the little monkey, had been abandoned by his relatives as they raided the peanut fields. Since then, he had been taken care of by Karamoko, the youngest of the Benfa family. But Boubouny, as all of his kind, liked playing pranks much better than behaving. Consequently, he often brought the old man's curse on himself.

The first few days after his arrival, however, Boubouny had shared in Old Benfa's friendship. The latter protected him from Mama Téné when he shamelessly drank her curdled milk, covering with dirt her carefully scrubbed bowls and gourds.

"It is your fault," grumbled Old Benfa; "if you took good care of your things, the little monkey would not touch them."

Now it was easy to understand the friendship the master of the house felt for Boubouny. He was the son, the grandson and great-grandson of a hunter, and Boubouny's presence brought him back to his youth. He remembered the days when he went through the lianas and brambles of the forest with his older brother Djigui who, now in his ancestors' village, carried on the family tradition with dignity. He relived the warm, passionate, and sometimes haunting atmosphere of the secret evening meetings during which the hunters vied with each other in skill and magic. Old Benfa even patted Boubouny, talking to him as to an old acquaintance. At times like this, Mama Téné would look at him curiously, smile and shake her head. The little she knew about Boubouny convinced her that this friendship was most fragile.

And indeed, things went sour the day Boubouny, leaping out of the mango tree in which he made his bed, snatched off Old Benfa's cap and threw it in the well. The lord and master, who was quietly talking to one of his friends, cried out: "What!"

His crime accomplished, the little monkey disappeared into the tree. Mama Téné retreated to her hut with a triumphant smile on her face. Old Benfa stood speechless, motionless in the middle of the courtyard for quite a while. Then he went to fish out his cap and spat out the most terrible insult at Boubouny: "May your enemies despise you!"

Since that day, Old Benfa changed his ways towards Boubouny. He spared him neither the slaps of his slipper nor insults and curses.

Old Benfa resumed his prayer after having armed himself with the heavy wooden spoon that Boubouny knew so well.

From the direction of the veranda, a clatter of gourds tumbling down attracted the attention of the solitary man. Mama Téné and Kany, who had just gotten up, were getting their gourds ready for the morning brew. After Kany *daughter* had greeted her father, they went towards the well.

"Well, it rained last night," said Mama Téné, picking up the rope of the bucket.

"Yes," answered Old Benfa. "I got up early to see if the roofs were holding up. Everything is fine this time."

"I think the little hut in the middle will have to be checked."

"The little hut in the middle is not the only one; we will have to do a lot of repairs this year."

Mama Téné dropped the bucket into the well while Kany put a big calebash full of millet beside her.

Old Benfa started to check his property, one hut at a time. He tried to figure out what repairs needed to be done, because he already knew the total effect he wanted to achieve in order to give an impressive setting to the great event to come.

"Every wall needs a fresh coat of clay," he thought. "The edge of the well must be completely rebuilt. I'll talk to Fadiga the muezzin about that. I hope he will not ask me any questions; he is such a gossip."

"I will have the courtyard swept every day for a week.

5

We'll put the singers over there, right beside the mango tree. The little monkey will go and sleep somewhere else." Old Benfa stopped near his daughter and gave her a long look. At this very moment, all of Kany's past unfolded before his eyes. He saw her when she was only a child, on Mama Téné's back. He saw her arguing with the health department representatives when they scolded her mother for having let the water sit too long in the storage jar. Kany was no longer the little girl who made everybody laugh with her awkward phrases, who tried to imitate the dance steps of the grown-ups, hopping with the agility of Boubouny. She was no longer the child who played house with other little girls, bustling about between the kitchen and the well, copying Mama Téné in every move she made. Now she is a big girl; very soon she will be a woman. Yes, in only a few days, she will be the wife of Famagan, the merchant.

Old Benfa was very fond of Kany. He told all the old people of the neighborhood about her knowledge. He told them how well she could handle the white man's writing and how easy it was for her to read letters, wherever they came from. Time and again, he had her come to the mosque, and there, among his friends, he made her read and translate everything he could lay his hands on. Then, he would say in a mysterious tone: "She can read what has been written by the machine."

But Old Benfa did not like to see his daughter in the company of boys who went to school. He became very angry when Samou, the son of Coumba, dared to ask for his daughter's hand. "Don't let me see you two together anymore," he had ordered Kany; "you will have the husband that I decide to give you."

Kany did not exactly agree with her father, and her opinion seemed to justify the words of the muezzin Fadiga, who told everyone who would listen that the school was the enemy of the family. The muezzin added that the

6

girls who went to school tried to make their own decisions, and that some of them even insisted on choosing their husband themselves!

"My daughter will never see the door of that place," concluded the muezzin, spitting out his cola juice[3] as he slapped his thigh.

While Old Benfa, looking at his daughter, was thinking of Famagan, the merchant, deep down Kany felt that she was bound to Samou, bound for life... yes, for life. They had repeated that phrase many, many times since they first met.

Kany and Samou had first seen each other at a fair on the river bank. Their eyes had met once, twice, three times; the next day Samou wrote to her. He talked of love and stars, of arrows of fire and of Kany with her teeth of light.

Benfa's daughter had dreamed as she held this letter. She had dreamed of the little house her European teacher used to talk of, the little house with its shining parlor and its heavy furniture. She had dreamed of the little garden where, in profusion, hyacinths, geraniums, and roses would miraculously mingle their perfume with the tropical fragrances. She had dreamed of walks along the banks of the Djoliba, when the dying sun would drape its golden shroud over the river at rest.

Kany dreamed of love and the future. She foresaw a marvelous future enhanced by the permanent presence of Samou. And often she could be heard humming the betrothal song that girls sing when they have made their choice:

If they put my head between two swords,
I will still be faithful to him.
The shepherd dreams of his star,

---

3. The cola is a nut much appreciated by Africans. It is often offered as a token of hospitality.

The boatman is faithful to the babbling of the river,
The bird greets the rising sun,
The child laughs on the old man's knee
And I think of the one
That I sing with these ageless words.
If they cast me with my hands bound
In the deepest waters,
I will still sing his praises.

Despite Old Benfa's anger, Kany and Samou had not stopped seeing each other. But feeling threatened, and fearing a trap, they turned to the powers they believed in. And so, after the blood-oath, they went to visit a sooth-sayer.

After listening to Samou, the sorcerer sneered loudly; then, without a word, he pulled two ribbons half a cubit long from a horn. He smeared them with *karité* butter[4] mixed with a drop of blood from the two young people and twisted a wick to which he set fire. Then, with a pierc-ing look, his forehead furrowed, and his arms raised, the man cried out: "With you the two powers of fire and blood, against you the power of death."

The soothsayer sneered again, uttered a whinnying sound and, without paying any further attention to the young people, started to chant, at the top of his voice, about the power of the night and the might of the gods.

Strengthened by this new protection, Kany and Samou became more confident, more certain about their future. They thought it wise, however, to avoid, when they were together, the places where they might be seen by Old Benfa or one of his friends. They often wrote to each other when they could not get out. Karamoko,

---

4. *Karité* butter is a solid white fat obtained from the seeds of the shea tree.

Nianson, and even Birama sometimes, carried their letters.

The Benfa family was indeed divided over this situation; Birama, Nianson and Karamoko sided with Samou, while Old Benfa and Sibiri, his oldest son, favored Famagan exclusively.

Actually the harmony of the Benfa family was all on the outside, and this Samou affair only brought to light a difference of opinion that had always existed. Very often, on the subject of school, vaccination, or something else, the young people did not agree with their elders, and if they did not loudly proclaim their disagreement, it was out of respect or simply because they feared reprisals. They laughed among themselves and protested sometimes disrespectfully when Old Benfa said that the red swirling dust carried seeds of sickness or that the scarcity of rains was heaven's response to the bad conduct of the younger generation. They laughed when Old Benfa offered sacrifices to avert tragedy in time of epidemics.

On the other hand, Old Benfa and Sibiri had their laughs too once in a while. They laughed when the young people told them that diseases were caused by creatures so small that they could not be seen with the naked eye. "And how were you able to see them yourself, then, you little liar?" said Old Benfa to Birama one day.

They laughed when Birama declined to drink out of the family gourd because it was full of these little creatures. One day Birama was beaten because he said that it was not wise to have several people eat from the same dish.

"My father and my father's father did it; if you feel the worse for it, go live with the white men. I put you in school so that you would be able to read. I never wanted you to become a white man."

Old Benfa laughed heartily when people said that the white men liked to take walks with their wives. "And who stays home then," he asked, "the dog?"

9

Old Benfa and Sibiri belonged to the same world. It was a world that seemed strange and barbarous to the young people. Born in the village where his father grew up, molded in the ancestral ways, Sibiri amazed his brothers when he told them of his childhood and of the principles which had guided his first steps.

In the village, young people are full of respect and concern for their elders. They revere the older inhabitants and everything that has been established by them. They listen to them religiously when they tell about the past or when they teach the lessons they learned from experience or from their parents. Never is there any discussion between the old and the young; life is entirely ruled by a single law, the law of age hierarchy, of experience, and of wisdom. It is only after residing in the "hut of the circumcised" that the younger ones are regarded as men. They are then supposed to have acquired everything that makes a man. They have learned to conquer fear. They know how to suffer and endure without complaint. They can keep a secret by resisting corruption as well as torture. They have learned to feel bound to their fellow men because "man is nothing without men; he arrives in their hands and dies in their hands."

But before stepping over the threshold of the "hut of men," the young undergo a series of trials. One can judge their worth and eliminate those who must still wait several years in order to deserve the name of man. Sibiri thought of those trials with pride.

A few days before the great event, at nightfall, Old Djigui had entrusted him with a message for one of his friends whose village was half a day away. Sure, they had given him a rifle, but Sibiri was alone, terribly alone on the little paths in the bush; all along the way, wild beasts lurking made his heart beat faster and faster with their hungry cries. Sibiri talked with enthusiasm also of the *Kotéba* sessions during which the young undergo the trial of the whip; the whip hisses on their back, dripping with sweat and blood, and woe to the one who utters the slightest groan! He is irrevocably rejected; a man endures and does not complain. Birama, Nianson and Karamoko opened their eyes wide when Sibiri told them that the youngsters, their chests bruised by the flogging of the *Kotéba*, have to throw themselves in the cold water of the river at dawn, come running out of it, and climb three times the sacred tree of their elders.

Birama shuddered when he was told about the trial by fire. The young men about to be circumcised must enter a burning hut and bring back an object that the older ones have left there. At the beginning the object is a pot or a basket, but the seventh time it is often a needle stuck in the wall.

After these important days of initiation, the young men are assembled in a spot outside the village. They live there for three months; that is where their adult life begins. If one of them makes a mistake, the entire group is penalized and the whip lashes accompany the ritual song:

Unity

I am nothing without him.
If he slips and stumbles,
I stumble with him, if I cannot keep him from falling.

They sing together, they extol discipline, they extol courage, they praise brotherhood. The elders stand by, ordering, flogging and teaching. Their every move is received with the usual respect because, as the song says:

They have preceded me in everything,
I will receive from their hands
That wisdom that I will in turn hand on
To those who will follow me.

"All this belongs to the past," said Birama to those around him. "Civilization requires something different. We are not made for the life Sibiri is talking about; it is good only for uneducated people. Today you have to be educated if you want to be respected. Look for yourself; the Whites respect only those who speak their language and dress like them, because only those are civilized. The teacher says so often: 'You two, Nianson and Karamoko, if you want to follow Sibiri's example, too bad for you! Go to an office or a store and you will see that the white men will treat you differently depending on the way you dress; they will show you some respect if you dress like them, but they will not hesitate to slap your face if you don't. The policemen will not spare you any ill treatments if you cannot address them correctly in the language of the white man. As for me, I have chosen. I will never let myself be outrun by the others.' They must assimilate to White culture to succeed

Nianson and Karamoko did not waver for long between Sibiri's primitive way of life and Birama's civilization. They chose to be modern and, like Birama, judged that Sibiri was nothing but an uneducated man. And besides, how could he guide them since he could neither read nor write? They sided with Birama and left Sibiri and Old Benfa clinging in vain to the past that life in the village represented.

Old Benfa, having thought for a long time, called Sibiri to his side. Breakfast was not ready yet; Mama Téné was still in the kitchen from which a thick, white smoke was now pouring.

"I would like to consult with my brothers Tiemoko, Moussa and Sori. I want them to be here at sundown."

Sibiri nodded and got up. Old Benfa called him back.

"We must talk today about Kany's marriage. Today we will give an answer to Famagan, who has been waiting for a year."

Sibiri, bearer of this heavy secret, put on important airs; he became grave and anxious. He, too, was thinking

12

of the great days he had just been told of. He, too, was thinking of the thousand and one things he had to do so that his name would be engraved in everyone's memory along with those of his friends who, on such occasions, had succeeded in impressing the people.

Mama Téné had arranged the veranda, she had swept the floor and scrubbed the walls. She had carried to the kitchen the old gourds and pans which usually encumbered the place. She had filled the lamp with *karité* butter and slipped in it a wick that she had braided herself. After all that work, she spread out the gorgeous mats reserved for special days.

Old Benfa, looking magnificent in his golden *boubou*,[5] had already settled down with his prayer beads in his hands. He looked so dignified, so imposing, that everyone coming towards the veranda tiptoed upon seeing him for fear of disturbing him. He remained in that posture, lost in his prayers, until the others arrived.

Old Benfa's three brothers showed up first; then came a stranger who made his presence known in the courtyard by jokes and colorful oaths. Tiemoko, Moussa and Sori did not seem very much at ease. Concern, and even anxiety, could be read on their faces. Indeed, gatherings of this sort seldom bring happiness to everyone involved. Most of the time, when all the men of the same family get together like this, it is because the wife of one of them has talked. There has been a complaint, and it often ends up with someone being flogged. As a result, Old Benfa's brothers were not without fear. Each one of them, pensive, seemed to search his recollections for a dispute or disagreement

---

5. A *boubou* is a long robe, the traditional African costume.

that could have brought upon him the wrath of the others. Several minutes went by like that, but their anguish vanished when Sibiri, very solemn, came and set a basket full of cola nuts next to his father. The sight of these fruits gave hint of a ceremony, probably a wedding—Kany's wedding; and on their faces, the alarmed look was replaced by a faint expression of joy. Sibiri's gesture, as it set their minds at rest, marked the beginning of the meeting. The cola nuts gave the gathering a formal character. All glances converged on Old Benfa, who put his carefully rolled beads in his pocket, cleared his throat, and turned towards one of his brothers.

"Tiemoko," he said, "God is great; may our will and his be one. I sent for you and your brothers so that we could discuss something together. Since it is a matter that will affect the interests of our family, it is imperative to get the point of view of each one of us. For almost two years Famagan has been asking through his compliments, his presents, and his many messengers to become one of us. Without respite, he has observed our customs. He has honored everyone of us; he has honored our friends and neighbors. As it is said: 'When one seeks something, it is with the hope of finding it.' Now, through the man you see here," and he pointed to the stranger, "Famagan asks us what we think of him. I am your guide, I know, but in matters of the future your opinion must come before mine. I am the closest to the Great Beyond, every year is bringing me nearer to our ancestors, and when I am no more, you will have the responsibility for all that concerns our family. My duty is to strengthen what is; yours is to prepare what is to be. That is what I have to say..."

After these words, Old Benfa took the goatskin snuff-pouch that Mama Téné had placed at his side, thrust his thumb and forefinger in it, and put some yellow powder on his tongue. He then offered the pouch to his brother Tiemoko and uttered a sort of clucking sound.

15

Tiemoko, now sitting cross-legged, his eyes lowered in respect, made no move. He looked at each one of his younger brothers, as if searching their posture for that special kind of respect that the younger eternally owe their elders. He cleared his throat, straightened up, toyed with the snuff-pouch, and decided to speak.

"We have heard your words," he said to Old Benfa, "but as always, 'the guinea-fowls look up to the one who guides them.' By wanting to be one of us, Famagan has made us very happy. There are a thousand girls in the neighborhood and out of these thousand he has chosen Kany. This action has a very important significance for us. It means that our family has been able to live by the traditions handed down by our forefathers. This is praise, praise addressed to you, Benfa. Famagan has brought honor to us in the eyes of the world. Thus, we are his servants. Our fathers used to say: 'I fear the one who respects me more than the one who threatens me.'"

"True!" cried the stranger. "Famagan thinks that too."

"It is not because of what he has given us," Tiemoko went on, "it is not because of his presents or the sums of money that we have received from him. Before Famagan, and even before Kany, our teeth were strong and we stood squarely on our feet. What inclines us towards Famagan is his approach, his very proper conduct towards us; in a word, his behavior, because our fathers also said: 'The best knowledge is that which leads man towards men.' Famagan has succeeded in winning us over; now it is up to us. Isn't it, Sory?" he called to one of his brothers.

"True, what you say is true; truth is the name of God."

"This is my opinion," Tiemoko responded. "However, my opinion is of little value compared to yours, Benfa; you are our master. And if the years are leading you towards our ancestors, their wisdom dwells in you also. We follow you as always and ask God for the favor of being able to profit as long as possible by your counsel."

16

Old Benfa could not doubt for a second the sincerity of this declaration. This was not a conventional expression used over the centuries, it was not a stock phrase uttered for conscience's sake. These words came from the very bottom of the heart; through them was expressed a state of mind formed by centuries and generations. They sounded a bit like a hymn. Taking back his snuff-pouch, the master of the house turned towards the stranger.

"Your friend is a good man," he said. "At least that is how we have seen him until now. It has been said that 'The panther has its spots on the outside while man has his on the inside.' However, knowing Famagan's roots, we trust him because we also believe like our elders that 'From the roots to the leaves sap rises and does not stop.' But he should know this: we, the relatives of Kany, are only carrying out a plan. It is God who leads. This being said, the day Kany arrives at his house, may he remember where she comes from, may he never forget how he won her; thus he will know how to act towards her. The day a disagreement arises between them, may Famagan know that 'The tongue and the teeth, made to live all their life together, sometimes quarrel.' Then, before coming to any decision, he should think hard: 'It is through her thinking that the old woman succeeds in changing millet into beer.' We do not want Kany to be thirsty while Famagan quenches his thirst. We do not want Kany to be hungry while Famagan eats his fill. If Kany disobeys him, let him guide her. But never should he consider humiliating her, because ridicule never spares anyone.... Kany will bring jewels with her; Famagan should never borrow outside the family as long as our daughter's possessions can be of use to him. Let him dispose of her jewels if hard times require it, but Kany should never have less than his other wives."

Then, addressing his brother Tiemoko, the speaker said:

"These are my words. Do you have anything to add?"

"No!" said the latter. "You have said everything. 'One cannot be taller than the wall by pushing himself.'"

Then the stranger started to talk. He praised Famagan's family and the one of Old Benfa and his brothers. After that the master of the house took the basket of colas, gave everyone a handful of the precious nuts, and they all shook hands.

Throughout the meeting, Mama Téné had not left the courtyard. She had kept, as they say, one eye on her cooking pot, and the other on the veranda. After guessing the subject of the discussion, she had taken it upon herself to keep the curious away. The curious who could have informed Kany; and by doing so, could have unleashed the tragedy she was dreading. It must be said that Mama Téné was much less optimistic about Kany's marriage than Old Benfa. She knew that Kany and Samou had completely disregarded the father's threats. They were still seeing each other, in the streets or at other students' houses. Besides, more than once, Kany had proven to her mother that nothing had changed. For instance, as she washed the millet around the well or spun cotton under the main veranda, she put Samou's name in all the songs that girls sing to their sweethearts.

Mama Téné had been a witness to shocking little scenes between Kany and some of her childhood friends. Every time Mata, Soukhoura or Koria came and teased Kany, showing her the magnificent presents of their suitors, merchants, clerks or shopkeepers, the daughter of Benfa exclaimed that she was not for sale and that she loved Samou.

Mama Téné also knew that Kany as well as her brother Birama treated Famagan's messengers rudely each time the latter tried to joke with them, as was the custom. So it is easy to understand that these wedding plans brought worry rather than joy to Mama Téné. She could see stormy weather coming her way; she could already imagine the tears and sobs of her daughter the day she found out that she belonged to Famagan.

After supper, Mama Téné was lost in thought. She wondered how to solve the numerous difficulties that would inevitably arise from this marriage.

Spinning her cotton as she did every evening, she cast furtive glances at Old Benfa. She would have liked to talk to him, to tell him everything that was bothering her at this very minute; but she did not dare to. She knew Old Benfa would believe that she was acting in collusion with her daughter Kany and that he would put the blame on her.

Reclining on his *tara*, a contented look on his face, the master of the house was gazing at the stars. The night was pleasant; the moonlight flooded the courtyard with a glow colored by the sky. When you looked at the horizon, it seemed that a skillful hand had sketched trees and hills against a vast blue carpet decked with stars. The tom-toms were sounding, covering up the quavering voice of the muezzin. Outside, the shrieks of the children mingled with the chants of the beggars.

Suddenly, the sound of flutes dominated the noises of the street. It was the call to the neighborhood young to come and vie with each other in the ancestral sport of wrestling. Mama Téné stopped twirling her distaff; Old Benfa sat up.

"The wrestling match!" he said. "The children are going to wrestle."

He lay down again and thought about his youth, about the exploits of his youth. He felt a bit sad thinking that the

21

popular wrestling of yesteryear was dying out today, scorned by the young who went to school.

Mama Téné, her mind distracted from her gloomy thoughts for an instant, hummed the hymn to the master wrestlers, and that tune carried her back to her days of freedom, the wonderful days of her childhood. But reality hit her; Kany had just come in. Mama Téné became anxious again. The minutes went by slowly. Feeling that her fingers had lost their usual nimbleness, Mama Téné stopped, got up and put away her distaffs after having brushed off the cotton threads that clung to her arms and clothing. Then, she changed into a better dress and went over to Old Benfa.

"I am going on an errand," she said.

But Old Benfa was asleep. Mama Téné stood, hesitating for an instant, and then decided to go and see the other wives, who were spinning cotton in their huts. She asked one of them to tell the master of the house where she was if he woke up.

Knowing all the worries Kany's marriage caused Mama Téné, it was easy to guess where she was going at this hour. Where did one seek quiet and peace of mind but at the sorcerer's? Yes, Mama Téné went to see Tiekoura. With his help, she was going to seek supernatural aid. She wanted to be told what offerings to make to conjure bad luck and gain her ancestors' approval.

Winding her way through the dusty streets, Old Benfa's wife often stumbled on a pebble or walked without a word past an old man who looked at her in amazement. Her heart was heavy with fear and projects. She tried her best to imagine the prescriptions of Tiekoura, whose prophetic voice she thought she was hearing. But Mama Téné was also proud of what she was doing. "If all mothers behaved like me," she thought, "families would never know shame and discord."

22

When she reached Tiekoura's door, Mama Téné could feel her heart pounding. She was a little embarrassed. Now she did not know how to broach the subject; she feared the eventual pronouncement of the soothsayer. She stopped, wanting to turn around, but having caught sight of a man who seemed to be coming towards her, she bravely stepped over the threshold of the entrance hall and entered the courtyard. In a low voice, she greeted a group of men engaged in discussion in front of a mound of peanuts, then she came to a halt in front of Tiekoura's hut.

Sitting on an old sheepskin, staring at the ground where cowries were scattered, Tiekoura was conversing with the invisible powers. Instinctively, Mama Téné bowed and greeted him. Tiekoura did not respond; he started to scrawl strange signs around the cowries without paying attention to her. Some time went by. Then finally, turning around slowly, Tiekoura scrutinized Kany's mother from head to toe and asked:

"Did you get up happy this morning?"

"Benfa and the children send you their greetings," answered Mama Téné, sitting down on a stool. They both remained silent for a while. Mama Téné looked at the strange things surrounding Tiekoura. Hanging on the wall were bulls' tails wrapped in strips of red cloth, statuettes, and masks with terrifying expressions. They looked like gods ready to change the universe into a great glowing bed of coals. They were idols in front of which Tiekoura's father and great-grandfather had knelt.

"What is the matter?" asked the soothsayer in a toneless voice. "I am listening to you, Téné; I see that you are worried, but we will give you peace of mind, peace of mind."

A glimmer of joy spread over Mama Téné's face; Tiekoura's words had already healed her.

"Tiekoura," she said, "when fire reaches the forest, the animals run towards the river."

"True!" yelled Tiekoura.

"For years now, Famagan, a virtuous and worthy man, has been asking for the hand of my daughter. Famagan is everyone's friend, I know; however, this marriage promises to be troublesome. My daughter goes to school. She has learned to judge things for herself, and, as you know, one can expect all sorts of things from children nowadays. I am afraid. That is why I am here."

What education brings

"You are right, Téné. You should be commended for coming to me. I am honored by your confidence."

With a slow gesture, the soothsayer took his snuff-box. "Tobacco helps the mind to see clearly."

Getting up so suddenly that he startled Mama Téné, Tiekoura took down two of his fetishes that were hanging on the wall. He brandished them, yelling strange words. For a few minutes, he stood as rigid as his statues; then he put the fetishes on a square of sand and donned a blood-colored *boubou* adorned all over with amulets. Then he placed himself in front of a mask with a diabolical face. All of a sudden, from an adjoining room, resounding tom-toms were heard; heavy, foreboding, with their slow, irregular beat. These tom-toms were not at all like those which, morning and night, gladdened young and old in the streets of the neighborhood. Hearing them, one could imagine a monster emerging from unfathomed depths.

That atmosphere, those masks with their terrifying grimaces, that sinister tom-tom, that strange looking, bold colored *boubou* sent a chill through Mama Téné. The tom-toms became louder and louder; Tiekoura knelt in front of one of the idols, then got up and went to get a gourd full of cowries from behind Old Benfa's wife. He spilled its contents on another square of sand at the far end of the little hut; he examined the scattered cowries at great length and pronounced a few words. Then, plunging two fetishes into a blood-filled gourd, the soothsayer cried: "Kill the insolent, protect the faithful, shroud of the living! Strike the indiscreet in the middle of his head, strike him and let there be no blood or pus, no fracture or crack, but may his head bear your imprint. Yet, protect the friends, and, if you have the power, I await you."

Mama Téné opened her eyes wide, her brow was beaded with sweat; she trembled. Hardly had Tiekoura uttered these words than the hut was filled with smoke and many moans were heard. The minutes passed slowly that way. Mama Téné, lost in her own little world, did not see Tiekoura, nor the fetishes, nor anything else.

At long last, the beat of the tom-toms slowed down, became faint, far-off, and finally died out in the darkness it had come from. Little by little the smoke cleared and Tiekoura appeared sitting, facing Mama Téné, swallowing his saliva. Three times he cleared his throat, and three times Mama Téné started. A feeling of impatience mingled with anxiety gripped Benfa's wife by the throat, but she kept silent. At last, Tiekoura made up his mind to speak...

Mama Téné went away pleased, her mind at rest about *hcunge* the fate of Kany and the harmony of the family. The next morning, she brought Tiekoura two gourds full of milk, a handful of cola nuts and a red rooster. Then, at the hour the sun reaches its zenith, she went out behind the town, and there, stopping at the seventh clearing, she offered twelve cotton strips and a handful of cola nuts to the first passers-by she saw.

Mama Téné did not breathe a word to anyone about what she had done or about what she now knew. She acted as usual towards everybody. However, a keen observer would have noticed that she had become even more loving and motherly towards her daughter. Was this Tiekoura's prescription? Nobody knows!

Old Benfa ceremoniously summoned Sibiri and said to him: "After the noon meal, you will announce the news of your sister's marriage to your younger brothers."

Even before the end of the meal, Sibiri had put on a sober and grave countenance; he had assumed an air of responsibility. After a few mouthfuls, he withdrew to his hut and sent for the young ones. Karamoko was the first to appear.

"Fetch Birama and Nianson." *Younger brothers*

Karamoko ran out and almost trampled on the little monkey who had crept between his feet. He came back a few minutes later followed by Birama lagging behind, as if he was coming reluctantly.

"Here is Birama," said Karamoko, "but Nianson is out somewhere."

"Come in," answered Sibiri, sitting on his *tara*, a look of preoccupation on his face. "The hand of Kany has just been granted to Famagan. Father asked me to tell you and to give you these few cola nuts."

Karamoko took his share and went away on the run. But Birama stood motionless, his hands in the pockets of his European trousers.

"What! Don't you like colas anymore?" asked Sibiri.

"Yes."

"Then what are you waiting for? Take your share!"

26

Birama stayed silent, his eyes turned towards the court-yard as if he was searching for some vague object in the foliage of the mango tree.

"Now, what is the matter?" asked Sibiri, irked by Birama's attitude.

"I cannot accept these colas," said Birama disdainfully.

"Why? Do you think there are not enough for you? If that's what it is, I'll give you some more."

"No, that's not it."

"Then don't stand there like that, speak up, say something. It concerns your sister, don't you realize that?"

"It is precisely because it concerns my sister."

"Then tell me what you are thinking, tell me what is bothering you."

"You want me to tell you?"

"Yes."

"You are sure?"

"Yes, absolutely."

"I cannot accept these colas because I do not like this marriage; I am absolutely opposed to it."

"What did you say?" asked Sibiri laughing. "And why would you be opposed to this marriage? Is it because you do not like to part with Kany so soon? This would not be very reasonable of you. You know very well that a girl is destined to leave her parents sooner or later. Moreover, the marriage has not taken place yet. Kany will still be with us for a few months, and even when she is with her husband, nothing will keep you from going to see her. There is no town or village between us."

"It is not that at all. I know very well that one of these days Kany will have to leave us. Karamoko understands that; all the more reason that I..."

"Then I certainly don't understand you anymore. However, I would like to know what's going on inside you. We are alone and this matter is ours. You have the right to speak your mind about Kany's marriage. Don't forget that we are destined to die before you. The day Kany has tears in her eyes, you are the one she will turn to. You are the one who will have to console and protect her. It is wrong for you to keep silent. If you know something about Famagan, now is the time to tell us; there is still time to back out."

Sibiri was setting a clever trap for Birama. These last words sounded gentle and friendly. They did not mislead Birama though. But seeing that Sibiri seemed prepared to listen to him, he summoned up his courage and said:

"This marriage will make Kany unhappy; that is why I am against it. Our sister does not love Famagan; she will never be happy with him. And then, he already has two wives. Kany loves another boy. Why would you oppose their marriage? This boy will be a success some day, you can be sure."

Sibiri burst out laughing.

"I knew you were insolent, Birama, but I've just discovered that you are crazy. You have to be crazy to tell me what I've just heard. What does Kany's viewpoint count for in this matter? We are the ones who decide; that is the custom. It's for Kany to obey. Since the world began, marriages have been made this way. You are too young to show us the way."

Birama's eyes shone with anger; his face became hard.

"So, that's the way it is," he cried. "Well then, since the world began, marriages have been poorly arranged. This is not even a marriage," he added, "but an auction. You're acting as if Kany was not a person but a mere sheep. What concerns you is how much you'll get out of the deal. You are giving her to the highest bidder, and now you don't care what is going to become of her. If she becomes Famagan's slave relegated to a hut among other slaves, you couldn't care less. What counts for you is what you will get."

28

"I believe that you have lost your senses, Birama. Besides, everything you just said fits in very well with your behavior, rejecting your background and being ashamed of it, dreaming of nothing but imitating the Whites, your masters. Yes, we have the right to impose the husband we want on Kany, because Kany is part of us. She bears our name, the name of our family. If she misbehaves, the shame will reflect on our family. This does not concern one person alone, but everyone. You talk about your friend, but let's see who chose him. Kany did, you'll say. But tell me, do you believe that Kany alone can judge better than all of us altogether? A marriage is a serious matter. It cannot be decided on by those who dream only of movies, cigarettes and dances. We know Famagan. We have made inquiries about him. He has his place among us. That is why Kany will marry him. You talk about the money he gave us. You know very well that we got by much before Famagan, and we did not beg either. And then, only Birama would believe that a man can be rich enough to buy someone's soul. The money symbolizes the effort Famagan is making to enter into our family."

Sibiri was unrecognizable. He was no longer the authoritarian free with his hands, but simply a man trying to convince his opponent in a debate.

"What is at stake here is not a name or a family, but Kany," Birama said. "She is the one getting married. She is the one who should choose. You think that things must stay the way they were centuries ago. Everything changes and we must change with the times. You know very well that, having gone to school, Kany cannot accept the status of being Famagan's third wife. If you give her to him, divorce will follow, immediately."

"That's what I expected! But tell me, doesn't divorce exist among the Whites? Let the Whites keep their customs! We will follow our forefathers. If some of our people dream only of becoming Whites, the future will teach them that 'a stay in the water does not change a tree trunk into a crocodile.' I do not know what they put in your heads at school, but you come back to us spoiled, insolent, and disrespectful. You pretend not to see the grown-ups in the street, so you do not have to speak to them. You think you are superior to everyone. The Whites are our saviors! But what have they saved us from? The day will come when we will make you change your tune, unless you decide to take refuge in the land of your masters, the Whites, slaves that you are!"

Birama was ready to scream when Mama Téné came in.

"What's the matter? What's the matter this time?" asked the mistress of the house. "You two will make me die of a broken heart. Two brothers of the same father and mother who cannot get along! What will become of the family after we're gone, if you are the ones who have to carry on? Listen to me carefully, day and night I pray for the unity of our family. Believe me, the one who is the cause of disunity will have my everlasting curse."

"Birama, Sira says that she is waiting for you and Kany at her house."

Birama departed with wrath in his heart, because he had not had the chance to reply to Sibiri's last remark.

In her hut, Sira had set up a large table loaded with glasses, soft drinks, and cigarettes; a record-player and a stack of records that belonged to Birama, "the musician with the nimble fingers," and Sidi, "the revolutionary," sat nearby.

At 4:30, Sidi put the record-player on a stool. The guests had not all arrived yet. Birama was strumming on his guitar. Kany, Sira, Aminata, and two other girls were singing. Samou was keeping time beating on the bottom of a gourd. In this group, three of the boys were always the topic of conversation, especially Samou, "the philosopher."

30

"How about dancing?" said Sira.

"All right," answered Sidi. "It's only fair that the late-comers should miss something."

They had hardly danced two or three times when Sira's little sisters came running in and said that one of the tenants was beating his wife. Everyone rushed out into the courtyard. The tenant had made sure his door was locked. Sira's guests exchanged glances. All of a sudden, Sidi, clenching his fists, started walking towards the little hut. He knocked once, twice, three times, and then waited. The whip kept cracking, the woman kept howling. Sidi knocked louder; no answer. He turned towards his friends and shrugged his shoulders. Then, gritting his teeth, he took a step back to get a better start, in order to mobilize all his strength. But the key had just turned in the lock. The door opened. A sickly little woman, her blouse in tatters and her hair streaming down, burst out into the courtyard. She sat on the edge of the well and began to cry.

Triumphantly, Sidi came back to his friends. They all stood motionless, their eyes turned towards the well.

"Just look at that! Is this marriage or slavery?" cried this righter of wrongs. "What kind of behavior is this? I've told you a thousand times, we have to do away with these ways. The way we treat our women will make us forever inferior to other people. Come. Let's throw out all these customs; let's liberate Woman if we want to survive. These customs are our weakness. If we want to go on we must become a strong people. It is Woman who sets society in motion. She is the one who makes it progress. She is the principal agent of our emancipation. Let us rid ourselves of all these worn-out things! Let us be a strong people. Strength solves every problem. Strength can accomplish anything! Look at the Whites. They talk about humanity, all right, but they settle their differences with cannons. Everyone defends humanity in his own way."

And defines humanity in his own way. . . .

Sidi stopped and looked at each face around him. None of his friends made a move. Sidi did not care much for silence. He found their attitude strange and even a little irritating.

"What's the matter?" he went on. "You're not saying anything today. Isn't one of you going to contradict me! Samou, don't you defend your customs anymore?"

Sidi did not understand. He knew very well that they did not all agree with him on this subject. He looked at them again, one by one. Samou gave a faint smile. Aliou made a face. Sidi sensed he was confronted with a concerted effort.

"You are a bunch of moderates," he sneered. And everyone laughed heartily.

If Samou, Sidi's best friend and number one adversary, had not said anything that day, it was because the girls, with Kany leading the way, had talked to him at the very moment the "revolutionary" was thumping on that door.

"When Sidi comes back, he will make a speech," Kany had said. "Nobody answer him; the girls want to dance."

small, but big moment

32

On their way back, Kany and Samou talked about Sidi and his lectures.

"I am glad," she said, "that you did not start arguing with Sidi; the two of you would have spoiled the evening."

"Anyway, we pulled a good one on him," answered Samou. "Sidi likes anything better than silence."

A cyclist almost ran Samou down.

"Ah! These people!" thundered Kany's friend. "When they have a bike, they think they rule the world. They have to make you feel as if they have something more than you."

"What Sidi was saying is not lacking in truth—all you have to do is look around you."

"I don't disagree. I believe Sidi is absolutely right when he protests against some of our practices, especially our treatment of women. But you see, the emancipated ones are not blameless either. The youth of today are known for their taste for luxury, their selfishness and vanity. Look, when they get together, they want to whoop it up. Heads of families leave their wives at home and roam the streets. In the offices, it is a bloody struggle to get promotions or to gain the favor of the bosses. The older generation keeps the younger from getting ahead. The younger competes savagely. Nobody cares about the children. People let them play in the dirt in the streets. What can you do in a situation like that? How can these people reproach their elders? One of our teachers said that we have brought the jungle to the city."

Twilight was slowly setting in. The sun was just a huge ball of fire trying to disappear into the depths of the river beyond. The streets of the native quarter were coming to life. It was the hour when the evening markets open up. Girls went by, unconcerned, their baskets of oranges or bananas balanced on their heads. In the hubbub of the crowd the calls of the market women could be heard from time to time:

"Oranges, beautiful bananas!"

Some women had already settled down with their large basins around which bees swarmed. They were sellers of lemonade or honey-spread. Merchants were coming in throngs from every direction. A few cyclists threaded their way through the crowd, ringing their bells. Small groups were forming here and there, and people could be heard arguing, laughing heartily, and slapping hands. A few men, standing behind long tables, displayed their cheap goods: jacknives, locks, basins, etc. The fish sellers were unpacking their baskets, spreading out their contents on mats.

"How unsanitary!" cried Samou. "How can they sell food spread out on those mats?"

Kany looked around and shrugged her shoulders. Samou took her by the hand and tried to make his way through a crowd of men who were blocking the whole street.

"Ousmane is crazy!" cried out a voice. "He is crazy to try to oppose me. I will spend one hundred, two hundred, three hundred thousand francs if need be, but I will marry that woman!"

"Did you hear that?" Samou said to his girlfriend. "He will heap his riches on the singers and the musicians. He will have the tom-toms beat for twenty days, just to marry that woman. Then, when she is in his household, he will treat her like a sheep that eats grass. What are we coming to?"

They went along without paying attention to the calls of the women or the gestures and words of the merchants who beckoned to Kany, holding up bottles of eau de cologne and brilliantine, boxes of powder, and those thousand little things which European women use to make themselves look attractive.

They came to the European section of town, which was almost deserted at that hour of the day. On the giant *kaïlcedrats* lining the streets, all kinds of birds—storks, turtle-doves, and chicken-stealing sparrow-hawks—were noisily perching. Bats darted around. Strange creatures, they seemed to awaken just as everything else was getting ready for rest and sleep. A few cyclists went by every now and then. Samou and Kany fell silent, as if they were afraid to disturb the spirits of the street.

Suddenly, Kany let go of Samou's hand and stopped, listening.

"What is it?" asked Samou quickly.

Kany looked worried and sad. Samou took her hand again.

"What's coming over you? Why do you stop?"

"I am scared," said Kany in a whisper.

Samou started to laugh.

"What a way to behave! What are you afraid of?"

"Don't laugh, this is very serious. I have just twice heard the cry of the bird of bad luck."

They looked at each other for a minute. Then Samou was worried too, but he exclaimed casually:

"Don't attach any importance to it; I just don't believe in those things anymore. It is superstition, pure and simple."

He started to sing, but his voice sounded different than usual. Samou tried to play the manly role in Kany's presence. Kany looked at him and tried to smile. She

Fascination of Europeanism

understood. As if by magic, the lights went on in the neighborhood and the whole street was filled with light.

"What a contrast!" cried Samou, happy to find something to talk about. "What a contrast between this neighborhood and ours. It's hard to believe that it is the same town. Here, at least, eyes are good for something. Look at these streets. They are wide and paved while ours...! Here, half an hour after it rains, the streets are dry and cleaner than ever. But when it rains, the streets of the native quarter turn into ponds and mudholes. When you think that the same city official is responsible for it all! Can you imagine? I just counted three lights in less than one hundred yards, and in our entire neighborhood there isn't even one. Something is wrong!"

bad-luck bird

Kany did not answer. She was worried by the cries of the *dabi* bird and the meaning of those cries. She wondered what misfortune the bird had just announced. Everybody at home was fine. Her uncles and their children were in good health.

Suddenly the headlights of a car shone on the two friends. Kany threw her arms around Samou and quickly pulled him towards her.

"Let's not go on," she said. "Let them have the road." They stopped.

"Do you see that little house, Kany? Do you see it there, right ahead of us? That's the kind we'll have."

Kany looked up; her face became radiant.

"Anyway, I'm the one who will choose the furniture," she said with an eager smile.

"Have it your way," answered Samou, happy to have freed his friend of the thought of the *dabi* bird and its forbidding cry.

And they talked of their future home.

Mama Téné was pacing back and forth between the house and the street. She was waiting for Kany. She felt impatient and a bit anxious because the muezzin had already announced the evening prayer and Kany was not home yet.

Every time Mama Téné caught sight of someone who looked a little like Kany or Birama, she walked towards them. She went back and forth like that several times, before her mind felt finally at ease at the thought that Sira lived some distance away and that children often forget the time when they are together, enjoying long chats in which everyone likes to put in his word on every subject.

Finally, Mama Téné went and sat in Kany's hut. She looked at the pictures pasted on the walls and at the stamps of old letters that her daughter had received. She imagined with sadness the way Kany would react a little later, when she heard that she had lost her freedom, that Famagan had won her. Indeed, Old Benfa had instructed Mama Téné to make her daughter understand that she was going to have to change her ways and adapt to her new status. From now on, she would have to greet the relatives, friends, and neighbors of her future husband properly and with due respect.

"Well, what are you doing here?" said Kany, surprised to find her mother sitting on her *tara*.

"I was waiting for you. I want to talk to you," answered Mama Téné without looking up.

37

Kany took off her shoes and sat beside her mother. They remained silent for a few minutes. Kany was worried. She was wondering what her mother could have to say to her that was so serious and important. She was on good terms with all her brothers and could not think of anything wrong with her behavior towards her family or neighbors. She really could not think of anything at all, unless a few trouble-makers had told Mama Téné that Samou was holding hands with her in the street. As she dwelled on that thought, it filled her with sadness and she lowered her eyes.

"Your father asked me to talk to you. Listen, listen closely and think about what I am going to tell you. You are grown up now. Thank God. Several of your friends who are no older than you already have children. They are happy and thankful to God. A girl's noblest goal is her own home. Yes, her home, a husband and children. This is the greatest happiness. You have gone to school; few of your friends have an education like yours. You can read a letter that comes from any town. You can write a letter to any kind of person. That is quite enough for you. I am your mother and I never learned all that. And yet, I have been just as good as anyone else, thank God...

"Kany, your father and his brothers have had a meeting. They have decided that you will marry Famagan. You must behave accordingly. On the street, at the market, wherever you are, don't forget that you are not free anymore. From now on, you have a husband and people will be watching you. This is your father's message to you."

Kany sat motionless, staring into space.

"You will have God's blessing if you obey the wishes of your family," Mama Téné continued.

At these words, Kany slumped down on the *tara*, and with her hands covering her face, she started sobbing. Mama Téné put her hand on her shoulder and said in a neutral tone:

38

"There is nothing to cry about. You are neither the first nor the last girl to whom this has happened."

"I don't love Famagan, I don't love Famagan," cried Kany sobbing.

"It is not a question of love," said Mama Téné. "You must obey. It is not up to you to choose. Your father is the master and your duty is to obey. It has always been like that." *tradition, you don't have a choice*

"Mama," said Kany, who had straightened up all of a sudden, "forgive me, but I cannot be Famagan's wife. Do whatever you want with me. I would rather die."

Mama Téné was at a loss for words. She looked at her daughter for a long time and put her hand to her chin in disbelief.

"How dare you talk like that? How dare you say such things? Is there a curse upon you?"

"No, Mama. But I must make you understand that what you are planning is impossible. Why, tell me, why do you reject Samou? What harm has he done you? Why are you turning him down? Why don't you let me go on with my studies? Please, oh please!" *education—thirst*

"Kany," said Mama Téné gently, "listen to me. You are not a child anymore. You can see and understand things. I have been unhappy in this house, I still am. For you and your brothers, I have endured it all, and I am ready to go on. You are my only source of joy. If you obey, it will make me happy and I will pray that life be kind to you. But if you rebel against your father, you will add to my suffering and I will no longer be able to hold my head up among my own." *— other mothers (her community)*

Mama Téné had tears in her eyes. Her voice no longer rang with authority, but with friendship and sorrow. It seemed that she understood Kany and knew that this marriage was a tragedy for her.

Her cheeks wet with tears, Kany sat with her head bowed. She felt twinges of remorse now. She felt selfish

big guilt trip

39

towards the woman who had brought her into this world. The last words of her mother had shown her a side of things that did not seem to enter her mind very often anymore: Mama Téné's suffering. Yes, Mama Téné had been neglected by Old Benfa as soon as he had married his two young wives. He had moved his belongings to his new spouses and had become a stranger to her. He did not joke with her or confide in her anymore. Kany could see all that now. She could see the two pretty new wives ruling the household. She remembered Old Benfa yelling at Mama Téné each time she argued with the more irritating of the two, Mata, the latest one. Yes, she could see it all now. She could see her mother selling grass skirts at the market, spinning cotton from morning to night, dyeing cloth, plaiting the hair of the women of the neighborhood, and all this just to be able to clothe her children: Birama, Karamoko, Nianson, and Kany too.

"Mama," said Kany in a voice quivering with sympathy, "You would not want me to suffer like you, would you? Then don't force me to marry Famagan. Let me go on with my studies, and when I become a teacher, you will have nothing to fear anymore. I will help you care for my little brothers Karamoko and Nianson."

Mama Téné put her hand over Kany's mouth.

"Don't talk about these things," she whispered. "Shh! Shh! I cannot help you, you know it very well. I am nothing. Your father is the one who decides. Compared to him, we are nothing, neither you nor I."

"If that's the way it is, I will never marry Famagan. He is wasting his time. I love Samou and I will always love him. But Mama, try to understand, I will always be your daughter."

Hardly had Kany said these words that Old Benfa burst into the hut.

"What did I hear?" he growled. "What did you say, daughter of the devil? Speak up! Say something!"

40

Kany retreated, but Old Benfa followed her to the back of the hut. Kany was crouching, her hands on her temples. Old Benfa looked at her, furious.

"What was Kany saying?"

"Just foolish things," answered Mama Téné, somewhat troubled. "Don't forget that Kany is still a child."

"You are spoiling her. You are the one who supports her degrading projects."

"How could I be spoiling her?"

"You do! You listen to her, you side with her. You even urge her to disobey. I understand now! It is because she is always with you that she has such an attitude. Tomorrow, I am going to send the two of them, her and Birama, to the village, to my brother Djigui."

"You are wrong to accuse me! But God is powerful, He sees us all!"

"Yes, of course, you hypocrite, God sees us all. Meanwhile, go tell your daughter to get ready and hurry up."

Kany, sitting on the floor, was still crying when Mama Téné came to her.

"Get up," she said. "You are going to get your dress dirty."

"Did you see him, Mama?"

"Who? Your father? Your father! Get up. He told me to tell you that you are going to the village with Birama tomorrow. Believe me, go. Accept everything. God is great. Put your hopes in Him."

Mama Téné left. Kany sat at a loss for a few minutes. Then she got up, stole towards the entrance and found herself face to face with her mother, who was coming back from the street.

"Where are you going?"

"I am going to get a few things."

Mama Téné gave her daughter a long glance.

"At least take your headscarf; your hair is a mess. Don't stay long. Your father might ask for you."

Once outside, Kany did not see anybody. She did not see anything. She did not even answer the greetings of the passers-by. With a slow, almost dragging step, she walked in the dust, barefoot, wiping her eyes from time to time with the back of her hand. Everything was changing for her. The street was not the same anymore. The tom-tom got on her nerves. The bursts of laughter that reached her ears had a grating sound. She was almost run over by one of the few cars that pass through the streets of the neighborhood. Some passers-by got upset and swore at her. But nothing got through to Kany. What did anything matter? Why live when you could not even be yourself anymore? This marriage would build a wall between Kany and her schoolmates. With Samou, she would have discussed, she would have given her opinion on everything. But among Famagan's two other wives, she would be like Téné and so many others.

42

Samou was reading an old newspaper when he heard a knock on his door. Kany came in, sat in an armchair right beside the table and remained silent. A little surprised, Samou looked at his sweetheart with a puzzled look.

"What is the matter?"

Kany made no reply.

Samou came closer and saw Kany's sad face and red eyes. He frowned, took his girl's head in his hands and in a voice mixed with surprise and anxiety said:

"You have been crying? What has happened? Did something happen to your family? Is somebody sick? Talk to me! Don't remain silent!" Caring, no?

Two tears rolled down Kany's cheeks. Deeply disturbed, Samou wiped them away quickly and crouched in front of her.

"Say something. Is it Mama Téné who is sick?"

Kany shook her head.

"Then why are you crying?"

"It has been decided that I shall marry Famagan."

"What!" said Samou, getting up.

"And tomorrow I will be leaving town. They are sending us to the village, Birama and me, for the rest of the vacation."

Samou stood motionless, his hands in his pockets, his eyes staring at the door of his hut. In the twinkling of an eye, his face had become gloomy. His eyes darkened and narrowed. Kany lifted her head, got up and came over to him.

"Samou, I swear to you, I will not marry him."

Samou did not say anything. He took a few steps and went and sat down on his *tara*, holding his head in his hands.

"Samou, nothing in the world can ever keep us apart."

Samou still said nothing. What could he say? He felt crushed by the weight of tradition. His heart was burning. He looked at Kany and felt sorry for her. Kany in Famagan's house! Kany relegated to a hut, cowed, bullied day and night according to the whims of her master. Kany alone with her suffering while her master runs around ever searching for a new prey! Samou wept.

"No, no," said Kany, throwing her arms around Samou's neck. "I don't want to see you cry."

Kany did not know what to do anymore. More than her father's words, more than anything in the world, Samou's tears pained her terribly, because for her, Samou was not like the others.

At that very moment, she would have done anything to her father, her uncle, and all those who were the cause of Samou's tears. They stood for a long time, Kany's head on her friend's chest. And the silence was broken only by the convulsive sobs of Kany.

"Are you there Samou?" the young man's mother called out.

"I must go," whispered Kany. "My father must be looking for me."

He loves the man-stance he tried to put on before on pg. 35
Now, he is as weak as her

Samou's mom

Mama," said Samou to Mama Coumba, who was pouring a gourdful of millet flour into the pot of boiling water, "something is happening to me. I was awake all night. I could not sleep."

His mother looked at him for a moment. She blew on the fire because the wood had not caught and the kitchen was filling with an acrid smoke which made their eyes smart.

"Wait for me in the courtyard," she said. "There is too much smoke in here."

Samou went out; he took a few steps and went and sat down on the old *tara* among the gourds and bowls that Mama Coumba had just washed. He patted the little cat who had come to him purring. The sky was dark; great clouds raced through it. A slight breeze was shaking the branches. You could not hear or see a single bird.

"Yes, Mama, something is happening to me," repeated Samou while Mama Coumba sat herself on a stool that she had brought out from the kitchen.

"What is it? I always told you to be careful. What is happening to you?"

"Mama, it is not what you are thinking at all. It is about Kany's family. They have found a husband for her: a man named Famagan."

"If that is all," said Mama Coumba, "don't worry. God is great." *Almost an indifference*

"But Mama, this is very important."

45

"What do you expect? God is good. If *He* decides that Kany is to be your wife, nobody will be able to stop it."

Samou looked down and appeared pensive.

Mama Coumba looked at him and became more and more worried. She felt that her son was expecting something else from her.

"And what about Kany? What does she say about that?"

"Kany cried," said Samou, ready to confide in his mother. "She came to see me last night. She was still crying. And oh! I forgot, her parents are sending her away to her uncle's for the rest of the vacation, to punish her."

Mama Coumba became thoughtful.

"Do you really believe Kany can make a good wife?"

"A very good wife," said Samou ardently.

"You know, your uncle promised me his daughter for you. You can find wives just about anywhere. Think about it and don't kill yourself over one girl."

"Mama, times have changed. I do not know my uncle's daughter. I have been going out with Kany for a long time. She can understand me. She already does."

"Yes, but your uncle's daughter will do everything you want. If Kany's family does not accept you, what do you intend to do?"

"We will do anything, but she will not be the wife of Famagan."

"You are really that fond of her? Be very careful, Samou. Women who have been to school do not fear their husbands anymore. They easily break up families, because they know and love only their husbands. Now, you know that a woman must obey, she must be patient..."

"Oh no, Mama. Kany and I get along very well."

"Yes, but you are not the only ones concerned. She must be able to keep the family together. She must know how to treat the people that will come to your house, and they do not teach you anything about that in school. For a

46

boy, all this may not be so important, but a girl must be well acquainted with these things, or else her children won't know anything, and their families will not be like the others anymore."

Mama Coumba spoke slowly. She was pronouncing each word very distinctly, as if she feared that her son would not get their meaning.

"Oh yes, Mama, you are right. But I have already talked about all this with Kany. You know her well! Doesn't she speak to you when you meet her on the street? Hasn't she ground millet for you several times? When she meets you at the market, doesn't she carry your basket?"

Samou did not understand that Mama Coumba could have doubts about Kany's good qualities. He was a little disappointed by his mother's reserve. His eyes were almost pleading.

"You are right. She is nice."

"Well then, you see that she can be my wife!" said Samou triumphantly.

Mama Coumba did not answer immediately. She stood up and said:

"I am going to take a look at the fire. Wait a minute."

Samou's face was beaming with joy. He had been able to persuade his mother, and this was very important to him. Samou had real respect for his mother. Ever since his father's death, he had never wanted for anything. Mama Coumba was always working for him and only for him. She sold the cottage cheese that she bought from the cattle-raisers, she had blankets made that she patiently tried to sell at the markets of the surrounding villages.

"Samou," said Mama Coumba, "if your father was alive, you would have married your uncle's daughter. But I will not force you to do it. I know that many of your friends do as you do. Kany is the one you love. You chose her. May peace and harmony reign between you the day she

47

becomes your wife. You lost your father when you were eight. The two of us were left, and you have my blessing. Kany's family may or may not want you, God will never abandon you!"

Samou listened devoutly to his mother's words. He felt capable of standing up to the whole wide world.

The compartment in which Kany and her brother were seated was crowded with passengers of all kinds: women carrying their babies on their backs, merchants dragging heavy baskets, soldiers, district officers, and so on. Through the door, Kany could hear people talking. She heard the cries of children and the last words of advice between passengers and their families and friends gathered on the platform.

"Tell him to trust me for the taxes," cried a man in his fifties to an old woman sitting near Kany.

"And you make sure to come and attend Salé's wedding," answered the old woman.

Neither Old Benfa nor Mama Téné had come. Only Sibiri was there. And what is more, Sibiri had been kind. He had chosen their seats himself and had put their luggage on the rack. He had forced his way through the crowd, when Birama and Kany were afraid to push. Now, Sibiri was talking with friends he had spotted.

Standing near the door, Kany was looking for Samou. And yet, she knew that her friend would not come. His presence would have caused more problems with Sibiri. But she kept looking for him anyway, so great was her desire to see him. The train whistled. Hands were shaken. Last-minute instructions were shouted back and forth. Sibiri quickly made his way through the crowd.

"Be careful, you two," he said.

Seydou Badian

In their compartment, Kany and Birama had as neighbors two dignified merchants wrapped in their cotton *boubous*, two young men about thirty years of age, a city woman with her forehead covered with gold ornaments, and an old grandmother lost in thought, surrounded by her old baskets. One of the young men got up. He went to stand near the compartment door. He stayed there for a few minutes and then went back to his seat, shaking his head.

"Phew!" he said, sitting down again. "Am I glad to leave this town. What a dump!"

His companion to whom he was talking nodded in agreement. The other went on:

"I told you he never knew how to write a report. He does not know the most elementary rules of grammar. I was the one who did all the work."

He pursed his lips and shook his head again.

"And besides, he hates Blacks; the black man cannot do anything, he does not stand for anything. Actually, he is the one who spends all his time drinking right under our eyes. You should have heard him yell at the attendant; 'Nigger! Good for nothing!' And what did the attendant say; what could he say? He has two brothers and a mother to support."

"The white men have come and spoiled everything," said the old woman who had taken her *boubou* off and had started mending it. "There are husbands here beside me, but they do not look at me and they talk a language that I do not understand."

Everyone started laughing.

"You are right," said one of the young fellows, "but what we are talking about does not interest women."

"Not true," protested the grandmother. "The truth is that we older people aren't worth anything to you anymore. There is the girl who interests you," she added, pointing to Kany. "If she is not afraid, she will compete with me, I dare her."

50

"I refuse," said Kany, laughing. "I will let you have all the young men."

"Now you see, she is afraid."

The old grandmother laughed and everyone joined in. A folksy family atmosphere ensued.

"If you want to win your husbands back," said one of the merchants to the grandmother, "you will have to buy some dresses and comb your hair instead of braiding it, and you will have to put shoes on."

"Me!" said the old woman, clapping her hands. "God help me! I will never tie myself in a bag. You call that clothing!"

"Then you will be a loser," said the woman with the gold ornaments.

"No. The husbands will come back to me. I am a good cook, I can plow the soil. I can also weave blankets better than anyone. What more do you want? What can these dolls do besides their nails, their hair, and their eyebrows?"

And everyone laughed louder than before.

The train whistled. A thick black smoke came into the car. The grandmother coughed a little and she blew her nose noisily. She cursed the cough, the smoke, and the train.

Then one of the merchants took a bowl wrapped up in a bandanna from his luggage.

"Food," he said. "Have some!"

The clerks, Birama and Kany copied him. They all brought out what they had. They washed their hands with the water from the merchants' kettles. They made a little group around the dishes of food, and each one took what he liked.

"My trip to the Gold Coast left me dazzled. I saw marvelous things there. I saw Blacks at the head of big businesses. I met some who were bank presidents. In all the offices where I went, I saw nothing but Blacks. Very few Whites. I could not believe it."

"It's the same thing in Kano, Nigeria. Over there, all the houses look like the houses of white people in our towns. The streets are lit from sundown on. The black merchants are doing business with the countries of the Whites. They are much richer than we are."

The others listened with interest to the two merchants. Birama and Kany kept exchanging glances. The clerks were also looking at one another and were shaking their heads. Except for the grandmother, who wasn't listening to anybody, everyone seemed amazed by what they heard about the Gold Coast and Nigeria.

"Oh!" sighed one of the clerks, "you merchants are very lucky. I wish I were a merchant too!"

Birama looked at him, surprised.

"Yes," the clerk went on, "my career was rough. I always had to deal with crooked bosses. And you, you don't even know what it is like to have a crooked boss. It makes your life unbearable. Whatever you do, he is displeased. He makes trouble for you, he yells at you all day long, and the office becomes true hell. If I had been a merchant, nobody could have given me orders. I would be my own boss, and I would not be bothered morning and night by a boss spitting out his hatred of my race. I work like crazy and any fellow fresh off the boat makes twice as much as I do. It is not hard work that pays off, it is the color of your skin."

"My friend," said one of the merchants, "maybe you made the right choice after all. You say the merchant does not have a boss? Believe me, he has several, he has thousands of them. With white men, you need papers, papers everywhere. You need vouchers, permits, passes, and heaven knows what else. We cannot read or write, so how do you expect us not to have masters? You step in an office; the clerk yells at you just to show you that he has power. You are mistreated, terrorized, and finally, you are forced to lay money on the table if you want peace. And besides, when you think of it, what can we sell? White people want to sell everything themselves. The millet that we grow, they want to sell it back to us; same thing for the rice and the peanuts.... Their goods, they sell them to the Syrians first, and we black merchants have to beg so that the Syrians will let us make a living. What profit do you expect us to make? When a white man is broke, the bank will lend him money. But who would help us? It is hard! It is very hard! The Whites support each other. The white commander is the brother of the white merchant, and a phone call can straighten everything out for him. It is hard! But you, you can read, that should have helped you. As for me, I am sorry I did not listen to my elderly father. I should have stayed in my village and become a farmer like my brothers."

"Tickets! Tickets!" called out the conductor. And everyone began to search their pockets. The old woman rummaged in her baskets. The conversation ceased.

"I see that you do not know anything," said the old woman to the merchant, as soon as the conductor went to the next compartment. "You are better off buying your goods from the Syrians. You don't have any problem in the city, and you still complain."

Everyone was staring at the grandmother. Unconcerned, she tried to thread her needle. But her hands shook and the jolts of the train threw her about among the merchants and the clerks.

"In my village," she said, sticking her needle in her braids, "any traveler who can read the white man's writing is a master. When the district chief comes around, everyone panics. It is the same for the clerks and the district guards. We work in the white man's fields. We produce millet or rubber for him. We work on the roads, and all that for nothing. Our children envy the city kids. They

53

education

think only of one thing: getting away from the village. Those who go to school do not come back, they do not know us anymore."

With a faraway look in her eyes, the old woman put her hands on her knees.

The second clerk, who was wearing thick glasses, said in a confident tone: "We complain, we all complain. But it is our fault. If we knew how to organize, things would be much better. Anyway, with politics, everything is going to change."

Birama and Kany nodded in agreement. The merchants looked at them, surprised and interested.

"And what does that mean, politics?" asked the old woman, yawning.

"We will have a chance to tell the white men what is wrong. We are going to tell them what must change in order for everybody to be happy. You must admit that the white men have brought us a lot of good things."

"No, no," protested the old woman, "let's talk about politics. Tell me, are you going to complain to a few white men? To the ones over here?"

"No, to the ones over there."

"But the ones here and the ones there, aren't they all the same family?"

"Why yes! I suppose!"

"Then you believe that the Whites over there are going to forsake the ones here, their brothers, for you?"

"No... but we want justice."

"And who is going to be their judge? The Whites?"

The old woman cackled sarcastically. She got up; the train was slowing down. The clerk looked at her with a glance full of scorn, but the grandmother did not care a bit. She collected her baskets. Birama and Kany got up and went over to the door. The train had just stopped.

On the platform of the little station, women selling fried fish, fresh or sour milk, yams, potatoes or roasted cassava moved back and forth, going from one car to the other, shouting and offering their goods. Some travelers were getting off, while others, with their baskets on their heads, were looking for a seat.

"May God watch over you!" the old woman shouted to her companions. "May the eye of the chiefs look upon you with respect!"

"Amen!" answered the merchants, while Birama, Kany, and the clerks started to laugh.

"Yes!" said the clerk with the thick glasses, as soon as the train started up. "What I say is true. If we knew how to organize, things would be much better. For instance, our businessmen would not have to depend on European firms and on the Lebanese and Syrians. They would be able to deal directly with the manufacturers in France. We are the ones producing the raw materials. Why don't we ship them to Europe ourselves? It is for us that the European goods are made. Why do our merchants have to buy them from other merchants? Our shopkeepers must have a chance to unite, to combine their strengths so as to be strong enough to fight the middlemen. The intermediaries are the ones who make life hard. Once these united merchants are strong, they will be able to create business schools with their own funds, and these schools will allow their children to learn business skills."

A traveler came into the compartment. One of the merchants, who had stretched out in the old woman's seat, sat up. The newcomer greeted them and sat down.

"In farming also," the clerk went on, "we need to get organized. We have to create agricultural schools. Then we will have a generation of trained farmers who will naturally oppose traditional, ancient methods. There are so many things to do, so many things to do!"

The clerk became lost in thoughts. He lit a cigarette and shook his head, implying by this gesture that he knew more than what he had said. The merchants looked

gold
lords

pensive too. They could already picture themselves as wealthy men, surrounded by friends, musicians, and poets. They could picture beautiful women adorned with gold trinkets at their side, and they could see themselves giving out presents and bringing wealth to others around them.

Suddenly, the other clerk sat up.

"Do you really believe," he said to his friend, "that the white men would let us accomplish everything you say?"

The merchants gave a start.

"Why not? That sort of undertaking would certainly be encouraged by the government," answered the clerk with the thick glasses, his confidence unshakable.

The other clerk burst out laughing, got up and went towards the door. His friend shrugged his shoulders. The merchants were looking at him, disappointed. Birama and Kany were disappointed too. The clerk with the thick glasses kept quiet.

The merchants began to yawn.

Birama and Kany remained lost in their thoughts. Nobody said another word.

The train came into the station at K. Birama and Kany got off after saying goodbye to their companions. Carrying their suitcases, they walked to the bank of the river. The village of Old Djigui was on the other side.

The riverbank was as lively as the evening markets in the city. There were mostly women there. They moved about, arguing, bargaining, and laughing loudly. A little farther on, the washer-women were at work, and there again, arguing and loud laughter could be heard. Wet fishnets were spread out to dry on the sand. Children, naked or barely clothed, busied themselves spreading out more. Policemen moved about. The boatmen kept busy. Some were fixing their old pirogues, and the sound of their axes could be heard time and again above the general uproar. Others were calling out to the travelers.

Still others were unloading the barges full of oranges, bananas or smoked fish. The women rushed over, trying to bargain. Birama took a place in a barge with Kany after haggling with the boatmen. Crossing the river did not take long. As soon as they were in the boat, the two city dwellers felt themselves filled with sad and uncomfortable thoughts. They had parted with their companions from the train, and those companions represented a bit of the city to them. Now they were alone, surrounded by people with whom they had nothing in common: boatmen with bare chests,

57

village people dressed in coarse cotton clothing. These faces meant nothing to Birama and Kany. They were completely foreign to them, and so the brother and sister took no interest in anything. They were indifferent to everything. Their surroundings made them realize that they were far from the city, far away from the thousands of things that give the city its charm. And so they kept silent and paid no attention to the boisterous conversations, or even to the monotonous chanting of the boatmen.

They disembarked on the other bank and followed a little path lined with tall grasses. They passed round many thickets and gigantic anthills. As they went by, the grass rustled. The birds stopped singing. Some flew away. The two of them walked in silence, their thoughts filled with fear. After a few minutes, they saw women and children gathering around the wells. They were the women of Old Djigui's village. Birama and Kany went towards the small group. The children who were playing a few yards away from the well stopped their games when they saw the two city dwellers. The ones who were sitting got up, those who were talking became silent, and all of them, motionless, stared with curiosity mixed with fear. Seeing that Birama and Kany were coming towards them, the children ran back and joined their families around the well. The women who had been chatting so noisily were now silent. Curious, uneasy, scared, they were all looking at these two strangers who, by their manners, could only be a government clerk and his wife. *Mis-perception of natives*

Motionless, they stood frozen by the edge of the well with their bucket rope in their hands, or even their calabash of water on their heads.

Birama, who was walking ahead of his sister, went straight over to an old woman who was standing a little apart from the others. She walked boldly towards him.

Grandma

"We are looking for the house of Djigui, the hunter," said Birama, trying to make his voice sound reassuring.

"There is no hunter by the name of Djigui in our village," answered the old woman in a gruff tone.

Birama and Kany looked at each other, puzzled. Meanwhile, a few children were already fleeing towards the village.

"We are the children of Benfa, the brother of Djigui," said Kany in a pleasant voice.

The old woman looked at them for a moment. She beamed.

"Oh my!" she cried, clapping her hands. "Then you are my grandchildren. When he was young, your father used to chase the monkeys and climb the tamarind trees."

The grandmother took Birama by the arm, turned towards her companions and exclaimed:

"They are the children of Benfa, Djigui's brother. They come from the city."

Other women rushed towards them with all sorts of exclamations. Every one of them was trying to put in a word about the kindness and good behavior of Old Benfa. Then the old woman picked up her calabash and asked the two city dwellers to follow her.

The entire northern part of this little village seemed encircled by the forest. It was not a man-made setting. The place had been shaped by the forest itself, with its life, its mystery and its legends. Thick bushes covered with thorns and birds' nests were in the foreground. Then came the tall trees with their few branches and sparse foliage. Around their trunks, a few had a tangled mass of lianas overlapping and trying to reach the tops. Still further away, there were gigantic palm trees.

The birds were there. Their songs blended. The millet-eaters swooped down in swarms all over the bushes.

The fields were in the southern part, spread out as far as the eye could see. A few children stood on makeshift platforms, holding catapults. With screams and stones, they were defending the corn against the wild parrots, tireless thieves.

In the East, the sun gilded the tops of the hills.

a page of info about:

In the shade of a tall tree, Old Djigui, sitting among other elders of the village, was sewing cotton strips together. He already knew that two strangers were asking for him. The children had told him that. Some had even mentioned specifically that they were "a government employee and his wife." But Old Djigui, unruffled, went on sewing his cotton strips together and spitting out his tobacco juice. The other elders, worried, wondered what Djigui could have done wrong, while the chief of the hunters tried to keep calm. He was not only a man, he was a hunter, that is to say one of those who can, with one swing of a club, put a lion to flight. But now, it was not a question of a lion or a leopard, and not even of the great beings of the night.

Old Djigui remembered that the year before he had told the district headquarters that he did not own a rifle anymore. His age advised against the trip from his village to the office of the district chief just to declare ownership of his rifle each year. But Old Djigui *was* a hunter. The whole village knew him as the son and grandson of hunters whose names were still recalled in the songs of the night gatherings. Thus he could not abandon the family tradition. *Oral tradition*

Old Djigui could do everything that a hunter can do, but it was against the beasts that he used his power. Among men, he remained a man. That is why he was not calling to his aid any of the supernatural powers which, since his great grandfather's time, his family had possessed.

61

Birama and Kany arrived with their escort. The elders who had seen them turned their backs on them. Old Djigui pretended not to see anything.

"The children of Benfa have come to see you," cried the old woman, twenty yards away from the tree.

Old Djigui straightened up, smiled, and held out his hand. Birama ran towards him.

"If you come to visit with us," said the old man, "you will have to wear clothes like ours."

Birama smiled. The other elders stood up and made a circle around Old Djigui and his niece and nephew. Greetings began on all sides.

"How is Benfa?"

"Everything is well with us."

And once more, everyone there told what they knew about Benfa, his kindness and his courage.

After everyone finished talking, Old Djigui led the children to his house.

Birama and Kany had met all their relatives. Some of the elders had talked at length about Old Benfa's childhood, spelling out the virtues of their father. They had paid a visit to the chiefs and the other important people of the village. Old Djigui, never tiring, had accompanied them from door to door, from hut to hut. He did not want to forget anybody, because in such instances, it was easy to make enemies.

"Well, he did not bring them over to my house. So I am nothing in his eyes."

The elders that Birama and Kany met talked of the city and of a thousand things.

"My son is over there, in the city. He went to work there to pay our taxes. The first year, he sent us some money; since then, nothing. Do you know him?"

"Mine was not very lucky. He could not find any work, and the white men put him in jail because he was not working. Is that his fault?"

"Here in the village, we don't have any money, we cannot pay any taxes. Our children go to work in the city to send us some money, but they do not come back anymore. Weeds cover the fields. Couldn't you tell the white men that we are in trouble? The young are not like us. They like the city better. They say that people are better off over there. They say that they are happier. Is that true?"

"Tell the white men that you have learned enough things, that they should leave you alone now. You are old enough to start a family. Become an official and come back here to protect us."

Even Old Djigui had said:

"The white chief comes to the village with his guards. He wants us to salute him, with our hand to our head. We are old, it makes us tired, doesn't he know it? In the next village, he put a chief who is not from here; nobody wants him except the white people. Our people are afraid, they tremble. Doesn't the white man know that when you tremble in front of a chief, you secretly hope to see him tremble too?"

"A chief who makes his people tremble is like a big stone which bars a trail. The travelers avoid it, they walk around it, but one day they realize that the way would be shorter if the stone was not there. Then they come, many of them together, and they move it. Force does not make a chief but an enemy to destroy."

"The white men force us to take off our hats to greet them. Tell them that here, an elder does not bare his head. Tell them also that it is the young who must greet the old. Before, village matters did not leave the village; why do they now force us to go to the district center, where the official insults us? Tell them that we are not happy. We will give them even more chickens, we will give them even more millet flour if we have to and if they want us to, but we are not happy."

K any was lying down on the *tara* that belonged to one of her aunts, but she could not sleep. The old woman had said to her:

"I am more comfortable on this mat on the ground. I know that in the city you do not like that, so I prepared the *tara* for you; you will sleep well there. Besides, why avoid the ground? Isn't it the place that awaits us all?"

Death

The old woman had laughed, showing her gums with only a few teeth left. So many thoughts were coming to Kany's mind. If Birama had been near her, she would have talked of many things.

But Old Djigui had said: "Birama, you will stay with the men." And Kany had found herself alone with her aunts and cousins.

Kany tossed and turned constantly, and now and then she sighed. She pictured the village, its small thatched huts, its storehouses with their cone-shaped roofs, and the smell of *karité* coming from most of the houses. She remembered the fetishes, the strange statuettes, the masks with their many tattooes on the low clay walls, and the courtyards where sheep and goats roam while the fowl bustle about near the doors of the storehouses.

She thought of the women, their laughter resounding around the wells, their cotton skirts, and the stories they told all day long, stories of the sowing season and the big fish expeditions, stories of bush beating and bush fires.

65

"What an existence!" sighed Kany. "The elders sit under the big tree, its trunk decorated with buffalo horns and fetishes. What a strange tree! Could it be true that, at night, it turns into an old woman and wanders through the village to choose those who must die?" Kany shivered. Old Djigui's dogs started barking. "What is it?" Dogs never bark without a reason. There is always something when a dog barks: an animal, a monster, a stranger or one of the great beings invisible to man. "Could it be the big tree?" Kany closed her eyes. Sounds of laughter came from the street. A little more at ease, the daughter of Benfa sat up and looked out into the courtyard.

"Everything is quiet," she thought to herself. "Maybe it is people walking by who make the dogs bark."

Kany thought of the big clearing not far from the tree, the place where the evil spirits of the neighborhood gather, and from where, at night, strange cries can be heard! Fatal cries, because he who hears them, his days are numbered. What a life!

She pictured the men of the village, most of them covered with amulets, marching by: silent old men with gloomy eyes, young men in their *boubous* of yellow cotton. No, this is not the city. Nothing here could remind you of it. Fire is made with a flint. Millet meal is eaten with salt. There is no sugar or money here, and you do not buy, you barter.

Women do not know any of the thousand things you can use to pretty yourself up so well. They wear their skirts around their hips; a few wear blouses, but what blouses! Kany sighed.

The elders forbid the women to wear beads, and Old Djigui thinks this is very wise.

"Yes," said the old man, "once a few merchants came from the city with their baskets full of beads. Every woman wanted to own the prettiest necklace or the most delicate bracelet. The women became envious of each other, and

66

the men exchanged blows. Then we decided: no more beads."

What a life! Kany rolled over on her bed. For entertainment, all they have is the tom-tom. Holidays? Sowing season, hunting season, fishing season...Then the whole village awakens; the elders lead, everyone is busy, from the youngest to the eldest, and the tom-toms pound.

The tom-toms beat everywhere, continually.

Kany started to yawn, disgusted.

All of a sudden, a frightful howling broke the silence. Kany tensed.

The old woman, who had seemed asleep, got up with a start; she put a mat across the door of the hut, made sure that the door was locked, scratched her back audibly and lay down again. The dogs did not dare bark this time. Kany, frozen with fear, hid under the covers.

The howling was heard again, and then an extremely loud voice thundered:

Totem of the dead!
Shroud of the living!
I strike the insolent
I strike without leaving any traces,
But where I strike, death shall come!

Now Kany was shaking all over.

The voice continued: Get out, the time has come.

Kany realized what was going on; contrary to what they said back in the city, secret societies were not dead. She burrowed beneath her covers and shut her eyes because she knew that death was close by. The horns echoed solemnly, and little by little they gave way to the doleful tom-toms. "It is the dance of death," Kany thought to herself. "O God, protect my brother and me."

67

Birama and Kany got up early. They were planning to go and visit a few of Old Djigui's friends in the next village. It was about seven o'clock.

Old Djigui was already busy making mats in his hut. One of his wives was grinding the millet, singing. Kany washed her face, brushed her teeth, and went over to the corner of the hut where her bags had been placed. She had hardly taken a few steps when she ran back, screaming, towards her brother.

"Birama, Birama, Birama! A lizard! A huge lizard!"

lizard

On Kany's suitcase, a lizard almost a yard long was resting quietly. Birama jumped off his *tara*, and both of them dashed towards the courtyard. Kany went to Old Djigui while Birama grabbed an axe.

"What are you doing?" cried the old man.

"There is a lizard!" answered Birama, his eyes full of fright.

"Are you crazy?" yelled the old man, holding back his nephew. "The lizard is part of our family."

Birama, his mouth wide open, stared first at Kany and then at his uncle. The latter deliberately turned his back to him. Kany took hold of her brother's hand.

"It seems to me that the white man does not teach you enough things," said one of Old Djigui's wives.

"No, the truth is they do not pay any attention to the traditional things nowadays. The white man teaches them the written words and nothing else," Old Djigui remarked.

"You should tell him things, then. It would be better if he knew everything," said the old woman as she turned towards the kitchen.

"Birama, are you the one who screamed?"

"No, I did not scream."

"Don't ever scream. A real man does not scream. Some chiefs only address their people by screaming; but you see, a leader who screams to make himself feared knows that he, himself, is lacking something. Did they teach you that back there?"

"No."

"Then remember this carefully, do not ever scream. Just never scream and never run away no matter what is facing you. A man does not run. The one who is living because he fled is only half living. He is haunted by the memory of his fear, or by his shame. He is no longer free."

"When you are facing a powerful enemy, is it not wiser to step back so as to fight better later? That is what Tiéman the Healer once told me."

"No, you must fight; fate has decreed it."

"Should you fight with bare hands, even against a wild animal?"

"The only weapon feared by wild beasts is courage. They all run away from courage; but when they see fear in your eyes, you are done for. It is the same with man."

Old Djigui continued: "If you are scared, it makes your enemy feel all the braver. Man must only be afraid of shame; he should never allow himself to be shamed.

"You have still many things to learn. Someone once told me: 'In the city, the children say *Me*. They talk of themselves all the time.' I laughed and I replied: 'We are doing something right in our village. When someone starts saying *Me*, *Me*, *Me*, we send him to the city. He no longer has friends among us.'

"When you are grown up, you will open your door to strangers because rice, once prepared, belongs to everyone. Man is a little like a tall tree: every traveler has a right to his shade. If nobody comes to your house, it is because you are like a tree invaded by red ants. The traveler will stay away from you.

"Tiéman the Healer once said to me: 'If you open your door to everyone, the lazy will be many.'

"But I replied: 'You will destroy the village with your words. There are thoughts that should not be expressed. We are like warriors on a battlefield. Fear lives in everyone. If we see our neighbor run to meet the enemy, we think to ourselves: he is crazy. But then we do the same thing, and we become brave. If each fighter had expressed his fear to his neighbor, we would have discussed the situation, and maybe we would have decided to flee.'

"Tiéman the Healer said to me about fighting: 'White men do not agree. There are still fights among them; another battle is to be feared.'

"I told him: 'White people are always fighting because they are on the wrong track, they tried to compete with the gods and they lost. To try to undo what the gods have done and replace it by what men want, that is the bold dream of white men. That is also the source of all their troubles.'

'If farmers, builders, boatmen, weavers and hunters all worked together for the village's sake, there would be no disputes.'

"'But there *have been wars* between villages,' Tiéman the Healer replied to me.

"Yes, in the North, it happened. Two villages wanted to compete to find out which one had the most fearless fighters. Neighboring villages became involved, siding with those that belonged to their families. The best farmers and the best boatmen died in the battle, and famine afflicted the area. This reminds me of what our elders used to say: 'The gods give their help to those who want to destroy.'

70

"'We must influence nature the way the Whites do,' Tiéman the Healer said to me. 'White men go along with progress, that is the right path.'

"'And where does that lead?' I asked.

"'Machines will end up doing all the work, and man will rest,' he said.

"'Man was not made to rest,' I told him. 'Without work in the fields, there is no good music.'

"'There will be fine houses, fair cities and fine cars. Everyone will feel good,' he said.

"Then I laughed and said to him: 'Go along with progress and troubles will go along with you. These houses, these cars, these machines, all these things will crush you one day and you will regret the village and the hard work of the fields, the chants of the boatmen and the movements of the weavers at their looms. Man must control his creations. If, through progress, you make the work of the farmers useless, you will find other work to do and you will feel worse than before. You think that with progress you will rule over nature, but you will only become prisoners of your own creations.'"

Old Djigui spat out his tobacco juice and went back to making his mats. Birama and Kany got up.

Standing on the roof of one of his huts, Old Djigui, his head thrown back, his neck tensed, and his cheeks puffed out, was blowing with all his might in a horn decorated with amulets. The women retired to their huts. The domestic animals, sheep and goats ran away. Old Djigui blew three times, paused, then blew again, a long, drawn out blast this time, rolling his head from one shoulder to the other. A few moments later, other horns could be heard, some very loud, others faint and far away. Old Djigui came slowly down from the roof and walked to the middle of the courtyard. He stood there motionless, his eyes closed and his brow furrowed. He cleared his throat three times, then walked with short steps to his hut and came back with a red rooster, its feet tied tightly together.

Two other elders joined Old Djigui. They were both wearing the red cap of the hunters and carrying in their hands, as a sign of their importance, a buffalo tail decorated with cowry shells.

The brother of Benfa put his right foot on the wings of the rooster and pulled out his knife. There was a moment of silence. Solemnly, the companions of Old Djigui stood beside him and stared at the rooster with deep, pensive looks on their faces.

Having exchanged a few words in low voices, the three men squatted; Old Djigui slit the rooster's throat and threw it as far as he could. The animal jerked about. The old

72

hunter chewed a red cola nut and spat on the spots of blood. Birama and Kany, dumbfounded, watched their uncle from the door of their hut. They felt overcome by a feeling of fear mingled with spirituality.

A few hours before the annual night of the hunters, Old Djigui had greeted his ancestors. He had offered them the sacrifice of the traditional red rooster with the ritual words:

"Accept it with our greetings. You are always among us in our huts and in the bush."

During the evening meal, Birama and Kany, whose interest had been aroused by the horns, were anxious to learn more about hunting and the hunters' lore. But now, thinking of the red rooster, Birama dared not talk of hunting. He still pictured the wrinkled brow of Old Djigui standing in the middle of the courtyard. The rooster struggled before his eyes while its blood, still warm, seeped into the sand. The two old men were there, and Birama saw them mumbling next to Old Djigui. That scene had filled him with religious awe. It was hard for him to imagine that it was the same Djigui who was now sitting before him, the same old man who was now telling jokes and who was the first one to laugh.

"If I ask him questions, he will become angry," Birama thought. However, Birama would have liked to learn so many things about the animals and even about "the Great Beings" of the night. Of course he had read books about "wild animals," but he knew that these books did not reveal anything important, and Old Djigui probably knew more than any author.

He recalled what Fadiga, the muezzin, had once said when he had caught Nianson mistreating Boubouny, the little monkey. "Be nice to him. In the forest, this little monkey is the hunter's savior; yes. The experienced hunter who hears his call knows that danger is near. The monkey warns the hunter of the presence of 'Ourani Kalan,' the panther. Oh! that panther, may it be cursed three times!" Fadiga had added, and he spat.

After a pause, the muezzin had continued:

"The panther does not have any friends; it kills for pleasure."

Birama had also heard what Old Benfa said about the hyena—the fearful hyena whose sinister call wakes up the entire forest. But all those who talked of animals and of hunting treated the lion with respect. He was the king; there was majesty even in his gait. Birama gazed at Old Djigui for a long time; his lips moved, but no sound came out. There was a pause.

Encouraged by the good mood of his uncle, the young city dweller said to him, without looking up:

"I would like to go to your gathering tonight."

Old Djigui's face became grim.

"No," he said curtly. "What would you do there?"

"I would like to go with you, like Sibiri, when he was here."

Old Djigui did not answer; instead, he looked worried.

"Yes," he said to himself. "You are my nephew, just like Sibiri, but you have associated with the white people. You speak their language and you have their manners. On the other hand, I am the master. If I bring you with me, no one will dare say anything."

Old Djigui also thought that his companions would admire him even more if he could say to them: "Here is my son, he lived with the white people for seven years, and now he has come back to us." He smiled at this thought and stroked his beard.

"Yes," he kept saying to himself, "I will tell them: 'He has been with the white men for seven years, and now he has come back to us.'

"And I will add: 'Soaking in water never turned a tree trunk into a crocodile.'" Old Djigui had nothing against the Whites, but he did not want anything from them, either. Like the other elders, he would have preferred that the white men stay in the cities and never come to their village. The white men want to know everything; they do not even forget your cows.

"How many children do you have? How many oxen? Do you own a rifle?" And so on.

The youth of the village had finished their dance. It was about one o'clock in the morning. Everything was quiet. The toads, with their endless croaking, were calling for rain. The river was groaning. Old Djigui, dressed in a bizarre fashion, came for his nephew.

"It is time, come."

The sound of a horn could be heard. It was followed by seven beats of the tom-toms. Birama had been coached by his uncle. He was dressed just as strangely as he. At the entrance of the hut, he kept repeating what the solemn voice of the hunter said to him:

"My eyes will see, but my mouth will stay closed.
Nothing about you will amaze me.
You have preceded me in everything.
May your power one day dwell in me, so that I can hand it down to the obedient child."

Upon these words, the hut filled with smoke. Voices could be heard.

"But..." Birama started to say.

Old Djigui started laughing.

In the twinkling of an eye, the smoke disappeared.

Birama stared curiously at his uncle. They exchanged a smile, and Old Djigui started on his way. Fear was already taking hold of Birama. But he felt somewhat reassured seeing the firm steps and the red hat of his uncle. It seemed that he recalled the words of the bard: "He who sits on the elephant's back does not have to fear the dew."

I am glad I met Tiéman," Kany thought to herself once she was alone. "He is really nice and he gives good advice. Besides, if he has succeeded in winning the friendship of Old Djigui, he must know many things. Oh! if all our elders in the city were like him, the young people would have wise leaders. Old Djigui likes him a lot.

"'This is my friend Tiéman the Healer,' he said to us. 'We do not always agree, because more than one path leads to the river. Tiéman often has the wisdom of the old. He was right, the one who said: 'The young man who has traveled to a hundred villages is the equal of the old man who has lived a hundred years.'

"Yes, Tiéman is a wise man. He is educated, he traveled through Europe when he was in the army. But for heaven's sake, why did Tiéman, when he was only a few steps away from his teaching certificate, choose to remain a healer in a village? He is certainly much better educated than most clerks that we meet in the city. Oh Tiéman! Why didn't I meet him sooner? He would have talked to me at length about the countries he visited. I trust him. He promised me to talk to Old Djigui. He told me:

"'I will do all I can with the old man so that you can go on with your studies; then, Famagan will look for a wife elsewhere and you will be with Samou.' Oh Tiéman! How happy I will be to continue my studies and remain with Samou.

"Samou, if you knew what was brewing at this very moment! Yes, something is afoot. If I could only write to you. But, from this hole, it is out of the question. The mail only comes every other week, and the letters people send hardly ever reach their destination. I could have sent you a message with a traveler, but since I have been here, nobody has left the village.

"I would so much like to know what has happened since I left. I would so much like to have news of the city. I would so much like to know what you are doing, Samou."

That young man is not well; a wicked one must have cast a spell over him. Coumba, you should talk to Ousmane, the marabout."

Massa, the fruitseller, had come to visit Mama Coumba. She thought that Samou had been acting strangely for some time, and the neighborhood women thought the same thing. They had whispered about it for a time, and Massa, because of her friendship with Mama Coumba, had decided to say something to her about it.

Indeed, since Kany had left, Samou, who usually enjoyed teasing the old women and listening patiently to their stories, barely greeted them. He stopped going to the places where his young friends gathered.

Mama Coumba knew very well what it was all about. She tried to talk to her son, but it was no use. Each time Samou answered that nothing was wrong and that he felt fine. He stayed away from the neighborhood life until two events occured that shook the city.

The first one was an epidemic of cerebro-spinal meningitis. It started in the northern part and gradually spread through the entire city. This disease, old-timers said, had only made its appearance in Africa during the war. They said also that the black soldiers had brought it back from the country of the white men.

"Our fathers never talked of it; it is an illness of the European era."

"The wooden neck," as the illness was called, was a real disaster for the city. A child would complain of a head-

78

ache, throw up, then die, and no one could do anything about it. Cries of grief and dismay multiplied, and the whole city took on an air of mourning.

The streets in the native quarters, usually lit by the little lamps of the fruitsellers, had become dark and gloomy; the women had left their stands. The tom-toms were silent too. The children who used to play their lively, noisy games after the evening meal did not show up anymore. The old-timers, puzzled and frightened, called it a curse because the disease seemed to affect mostly the young.

"We are cursed," the old people said. "The ones who were to bury us, die before us. What will become of us?"

An oppressive silence hung over the city, interrupted from time to time by a distressing choir of weeping women. Death spread from door to door, each family passively awaiting its turn. Offerings were made, public prayers were organized, and that evening the voice of Fadiga, the muezzin, had an especially heart-rending tone. All the elders were there, pensive, their faces lined with anguish. On the top of the mosque stood the white-clad figure of Fadiga. There was something godlike about him. To be sure, his words were the same as on other days, but in his voice, you could sense something deep, and his words carried the breath of a last hope. All the elders were praying and calling upon God. They were not afraid to die, those old people. They had already witnessed many, many things, and so, on that evening, they asked the Almighty to strike down the old rather than the young, to guide the disease towards those who had already known youth and wisdom and to spare the ones who bore on their shoulders the responsibilities of the days to come. In this manner, the order of things would be respected.

Samou had come out of his shell. The elders were constantly asking him for explanation about this strange illness. They asked him how to protect themselves from it. However, Samou, who did not know much on this subject, limited himself to telling them what he knew from school:

79

that the illness was caused by a germ and that they should sprinkle the floors of their huts with water before sweeping.

After having satisfied its ghoulish desires, the evil spirit of the cerebro-spinal disease departed, leaving in its wake mourning and despair.

The second event had been brewing for a long time already. It was first reported by the soldiers who had returned from the war.

"Soon, everyone will be a citizen," they said. "They talked to us up there. There will be no more forced labor. In the army, there will no longer be differences between soldiers. They will all be dressed alike, and they will all have a right to equal treatment. The schools will be the same for all the children, black and white. Justice also will be the same for everyone, and nobody will go to prison without a trial. Soon, all will be well."

People held on to this news, but the elders, who said they had heard that kind of rumor before, remained skeptical. Their attitude was very different from the enthusiasm expressed by the young. The latter discussed the words of the soldiers over and over again. It was all so wonderful...

There was some excitement in the city, then people stopped talking about it, and it was forgotten.

As soon as the meningitis epidemic subsided, the first travelers from the West brought news of deep changes. A few government clerks confirmed them this time, and people became excited again.

In the market place, in front of the stores and in the squares, people discussed the matter with wild gestures. They got all worked up about it.

In the offices, it was the only subject of conversation, to be sure. Some employees claimed that they had read of the good news in the newspapers.

People got more and more enthusiastic. The young people in the dance halls, the women on their way to the market and even the elders in their own groups talked about it. Wherever people met, all they discussed were the days to come, without forced labor, days of freedom and justice.

One Sunday morning, in the main square of the neighborhood, a meeting took place. The crowd became more and more restless, bigger and bigger. They talked of the days of suffering and poverty whose end was in sight, and everyone told his neighbor about his own particular hardships. All the whispering together formed some kind of muffled rumbling. It was obvious that these people were waiting for something. Suddenly, as if by magic, there was a deep silence. Everyone looked up. Makhan, a young man of the district, had just climbed on a roof and was facing the crowd.

"We are for justice and equality!" he shouted. "We will no longer accept being underlings forever. We will no longer accept one law for the Whites and another one for the Blacks. We will no longer be ruled!"

It is the thunderbolt. It has been said out loud; everyone looks around him, nobody moves. The police are there and they don't make one single gesture towards Makhan; they listen and they agree too. Is it possible? To say such things out loud!

But still nothing happens, nobody moves. Makhan is there, he is not in prison. Well now, times have changed, make no mistake about it!

"Equal pay for equal work. We have had enough of working for nothing. We want justice!"

The crowd is roaring, hands and faces are reaching out towards Makhan.

Makhan has spoken. He has said aloud what only yesterday was said privately between brothers, and nothing has happened. Makhan is a man. Times have changed.

A new era! A new era! The villager who had taken refuge in the city thinks of going back to his home because forced labor is going to end and from now on he will be protected by the law. He becomes a free man. The employee is happy. He will no longer be the perennial underling. He will get the salary he deserves. Young people will have the opportunity to study what they like. They will no longer be restricted. The soldier will serve under the same conditions as the white soldier. Yes, everybody will be fine. The tom-tom pounds louder than ever.

Sidi had run to Samou's place. "Come on," he had said, "the time has come." They had listened with enthusiasm to the voice of Makhan. Beside Sidi, a white man was listening, smoking his pipe. It was Mr. Donzano, their former school principal. After the speech, Mr. Donzano turned towards his former students.

"Hello, young men."

"Hello, sir."

"Did you hear?"

"Yes, sir."

"What do you think of it?"

"Well..."

"He is right, I agree with him."

Surprise on the part of Sidi and Samou.

"You should come over to my place," Mr. Donzano continued. "We will discuss all this."

Really, everything has changed. It is the first time Mr. Donzano speaks to his students with such informality. They are talking of electing representatives.

"You see, young men, I agree entirely with Mr. Makhan, but I think we ought to go slowly. Let's not rush things."

"Sir, it is a question of life or death. People are suffering..."

"Indeed, many mistakes need to be corrected, but they talk of setting up assemblies here. Isn't this too soon?"

"But sir, we have always had assemblies in Africa. There was not only anarchy and slavery before the coming of the Europeans."

"I agree, but our methods are completely new to you."

"Yes, but it is wrong to want to impose your methods here; at that rate, it would take centuries. True, we did not have any machines before the coming of the Europeans, but there was a social structure."

"Yes, I agree, but tell me, what does the older generation want?"

Mr. Donzano took out a notebook and a pencil.

"You see, sir, before the Europeans came, the elders used to have their say in matters concerning the village; in addition to the chief, we had a council of important people. Today, we only have a chief, and he receives and carries out the orders of the white administrator."

"Yes, but the elders are illiterate. How do you expect them to run the affairs of the village?"

"The chief is also illiterate most of the time, sir. Besides, although the elders may not be able to read, they understand the needs of their communities better than anyone else. Why couldn't we set up councils of leading elders and, to each of these councils, add one representative of the government to take care of the modern problems. We ought to have a share in the administration of the cities and villages.

"Forced labor must be abolished so that we can get along together. Discrimination must end."

"I agree; you can count on me. I have always had a high opinion of you. Tell everyone that I am your friend."

"You see what I told you, Samou. Everything is going to change now; we will know the good life at last."

Sidi was talking, waving his arms. He stood in the middle of the street making plans. He was talking about his studies. But Samou was less enthusiastic; he was thinking of Kany. Sidi finally realized it.

"Don't worry," he said to him, "Old Benfa will understand, now, that the future is on your side. Famagan will surely be frightened, you'll see."

"Sidi might be right," thought Samou, when he was alone back home. "Old Benfa will realize that times have changed. He will understand that I can become somebody. Everything will work out. Oh, if I could only tell Kany the good news, if I could only talk to her about all this, how happy she would be!"

I came to get you. I am taking you to the tom-tom ceremony. Today, we start the preliminaries of the third dance: the festival of the boatmen."

Tiéman talked while Kany stared at him. Birama was chatting with Old Djigui. The sky was as blue as the river at twilight. The untiring moon ran away from the clouds.

The wailing cries of the hyena, the most fearful of animals, could be heard in the distance.

A few women, covered with *karité* butter from the waist up, walked past Tiéman and his friends, laughing.

A roaring was heard. Sheep and goats, grazing near the low walls of the houses, became frightened and scattered.

"The bush is yours, O golden mane whom the rifle of the hunter envies!"

Birama and Kany turned around. A few yards away from them stood the person who had just said these words, a little old man in rags, holding a small guitar in his hands; it was a sort of gourd, covered with a lizard skin, across which some horse hairs were stretched. The lion roared again, and the little old man, his face beaming, his nostrils flaring, went on:

"The king has his sceptre but you have your mane, and your gait is as beautiful as the royal dance."

A pile of wood flared up, crackling, in the middle of the circle made by the noisy, enthusiastic crowd. The tom-toms were not beating yet. The women, getting impatient, were singing and dancing. The air was filled with a longing for rhythm and a yearning for motion! Suddenly, a bare-chested man wearing a strange mask advanced into the middle of the circle leading a he-goat which could hardly make its way through the crowd. Silence fell as if by magic. The man faced the tom-toms and put his foot on the animal's rope. He raised his hands to the sky, turned towards the women, repeated the same gesture, and left the scene. Right after, hands began clapping. Horns were blown. The ground seemed to tremble, the trees shook, the flutes whistled, and the drums rumbled. All these instruments combining their sounds announced to the neighboring villages the preliminaries of the third dance.

Half a dozen girls came forward, dancing. Half a dozen boys walked towards them. Around the fire, dark figures were moving, dark faces were beaming, lit by the moon and joyous smiles.

"You don't have *that* in the city," said Tiéman with childish pride.

"I never went to the tom-tom ceremony," Birama answered without taking his eyes off the dance and the dancers.

"Why?"

"Hum...well..."

"Oh yes!... I can see, it does not interest you. You are not the only one either, all young moderns are like you."

Tiéman came closer and put his hand on his friend's shoulder.

"Well, friend, you are wrong. We have beautiful dances and very fine music."

Birama acted surprised. He looked at Tiéman without saying a word.

"Oh yes!" the healer continued. "You are wrong to want to abandon everything. You are wrong to try to copy the Europeans in everything. Try to understand me. The European man is only one of the many facets of man.

86

Nobody is asking you to be European. Nobody is asking you to change your appearance."

Birama tried to get in a word, but Tiéman did not let him.

"You should not run away from your environment. Instead, you should try to affect it. Try to save what must be saved, and strive to contribute something yourself to the others: a face carved in ebony, the dazzling scenery of our countryside on a painter's canvas!"

Tiéman forgot the tom-tom. He uttered these last words with a special warmth. Then he filled his clay pipe and struck a match.

"You shouldn't accept everything, of course; but make a choice. Customs are made to serve men, not at all to enslave them. Be realistic; break all that enslaves man and keeps him from going forward. If you really love your people, if your claims of love are not born out of self interest, you will have the courage to fight all their weaknesses, you will have the courage to praise all their strengths.

"I was like you. When I was your age, I did not know anything about all that. But believe me, one day I realized my foolishness. I was a soldier in Europe at that time. There had been a party in our regiment; they had asked us to put on an act, typically African. I did not know anything about the dances or the songs of my country, and I was not the only one either; almost all my friends who had been to school were in the same boat. The Whites danced: lawyers, teachers, engineers, physicians, they all dressed in their regional costumes and they sang in their dialects.

"We stood there feeling shame, and what's worse is that we were ashamed to tell the Whites that we knew nothing of our culture.

"Fortunately, we were not the only representatives of Africa; there were some other soldiers. The ones we contemptuously called the know-nothings. We were proud of

87

them that day; proud to see them leap, faces beaming, to the rhythm of the drums. We had the feeling that they, at least, were bringing something to the Europeans. We had the feeling that our country was alive because of them.

"Without them, what would we have done? We could have danced European dances maybe! That evening made me understand the truth. Mankind would be truly poor if we all turned into Europeans. It is desirable in such gatherings that everyone be able to contribute his special song, his special dance."

Birama listened, at the same time watching every single step of the dance. The tom-toms slowed down. He turned towards Tiéman.

"Is this the end?"

"No, it is only the beginning. Now the elders are going to do their own dance; you will see the parade of the masters of the group. Listen!"

The tom-toms started again on a different rhythm, and the entire crowd knelt.

An old man, armed with a hoe, walked towards the scene.

"The farmers," whispered Tiéman.

The tom-toms beat softly, and the old man walked to the middle of the circle. He threw his hoe into the air and lifted his arms to the sky. The tool began to spin as if handled by invisible hands.

"Incredible!" cried Birama to his sister. "Did you see that?"

The tom-toms rumbled. The old man picked up his hoe, threw it in the air seven times and yelled once more. Everyone looked up. The hoe did not come down, and while the eyes seemed to scan the sky for it, the old man went and kneeled, motionless, in front of the tom-toms. He stood up, a few moments later, with the hoe on his shoulder.

"Fantastic!" cried Birama.

Murmurs could be heard among the spectators.

Small, resounding tom-toms announced the weavers. A tall, lean man appeared, a loincloth in his hand. The tom-toms beat softly.

All by itself, the loincloth gathered in a ball, twisted and spread out at its master's command. Birama was speechless; it was no use! He could not refrain from showing his surprise when, with the horns blowing, Old Djigui appeared in his hunter's costume, holding his rifle.

"It is him, it is him," he said to Kany. "Look at him."

Letter from Tiéman to Samou

Dear Samou,

Without ever having met you, I have been led to play a part in your life. I am sure Kany has talked to you about me.... I have seen Old Djigui. I have spoken to him. He has decided to speak to Benfa so that Kany can go on with her studies. Now, if Kany continues her studies, you will become her husband. So this is settled.

I have learned that you are a brilliant young man. I want you to know that Kany is a deserving girl also. Both of you have touched on one of the most important problems in our country. But remember this: your parents are in no way trying to do you harm. The sense of family is stronger with us than with any other people. If there are conflicts between our elders and ourselves, it is because, in a way, we represent two different worlds. Compromise is possible, but you have to initiate it. We have lived cut off from our world. We have blamed it for not having given us machines or modern buildings. However, machines and buildings are not everything in life. There are moral values also, and this is what shapes man. You will soon experience this with the coming of a new era. Man is not only the one who creates but also the one whose work plays a part in the building of the family of man. Technical knowledge cannot become a measure of superiority. In a way, it is only a will, an orientation, a need. New problems are being posed for us. We must restore a balance which was destroyed by moral blindness and the pursuit of selfish interests. Have the courage to forge ahead. We are believers; with us, fervor is possible, and brotherhood is a reality. Go forth with our values, go forth courageously and say "no" to hate, because if it is in hate that you find your fervor, when hate disappears, you will be an extinct people!

Tiéman

TL;DR: Don't throw the baby out with the bath water.

advantages of advancement,
but technical knowledge
not a measure of superiority
└ moral calculus

The day of departure arrived. On that day, the sun seemed to rise earlier than usual, the air was cooler and more hospitable. The day before, the young people of the village had danced in Old Djigui's courtyard. The tom-tom had resounded in honor of Birama and Kany. Presents filled their huts.

Led by Old Djigui, Birama and Kany had gone as on the first day, to greet the chief and the other important people of the village.

Kany had waited in vain for a word from Tiéman, a word about Samou and Old Djigui. Tiéman had not said anything except for things that had no connection with her anguish. And the daughter of Benfa had wept. Now, on the bank of the river, the young city people were waiting for Tiéman amidst a group of villagers. Kany kept her eyes on the path leading to the clinic. She was talking to Birama, but actually, she did not know what she was saying. She was waiting, and every minute increased her despair, heightened her pain. Finally, Tiéman came running.

"Oh, I have something for you, Kany."

Tiéman pulled from his pocket a letter that he held out to Kany.

"One of my friends, who comes from the city, gave me this for you."

Kany,   Victory letter;

News ... and good news.

Mama Téné came to our house the day before yesterday. She talked to my mother. Here is what was said:

Your uncle Djigui has written to Old Benfa and asked him to let you continue your studies, to let you go to school until you become what you want to be; he wants this to be.

Old Benfa gave the message to Famagan. The latter answered that he was not going to spend his life waiting for one girl when there are thousands of them in the city. He almost got in a fight with Sibiri. That is not all. Your uncle added:

"It is in the order of things that the girl who swims well be given to a good boatman."

Ah! Kany! You! Freedom! I seem to see it written in star letters on the roof of the world, that life goes on.

Kany threw her arms around Tiéman and cried.

The letter from Samou made joy flow into Kany's heart. It was as if the whole world was smiling at her. Nature, in her eyes, was clothed in happiness.

In the barge bringing her across the river, Kany daydreamed. She was talking to Samou, they were laughing with delight at their wonderful future. Nothing barred their way anymore. The plans they were making for the future this time seemed already partly come true.

The boat moved slowly; at least Kany thought so. The boatmen sang monotonously and the water murmured around their long, greenish poles. In the distance, the teal fled, while the curious egret followed that black shape gliding gently over the water's surface.

A woman stood up, leaned against the side of the boat and looked at the shore which receded, growing smaller.

She leaned over the side and caught some water in the hollow of her cupped hand. She let it filter through her fingers and repeated the same gesture several times, then softly sang:

> You who hear me, O Djoliba,
> Show me the way.
> In you all is strength for in you all is wisdom.
> O you are the same and your laugh is the same.
> Faithfulness, flow, flow, towards the rendezvous.
> Faithfulness, flow, flow, to your destiny.
> How many have seen you and see you still!
> How many have not seen you and yet sense you.
> You have chosen your way, unflagging, you follow it.
> At the rock in your path, you smile.
> At the boatman, your guide, you smile.
> You can be as spirited as the sparrowhawk,
> Yet reveal the wisdom of your years.
> Teach me, O river of my fathers,
> Teach me, O Djoliba, teach me to be true.
> In the days of light, teach me,
> O miracle, faithfulness in the days without stars.
> My heart beseeches you, teach me to be true.

Kany had tears in her eyes. She turned towards the singer and smiled. The singer stood there for a few minutes, then she sighed and went back to her place. Kany looked at her and smiled again. Without a word, the singer cupped her hands around her mouth:

> What will become of me now?
> What will become of me, O my Master?
> Ever since you left,
> The sun has lost its warmth,
> The bird has lost its song,
> My voice falters and betrays me,
> As tears fill my eyes.

"I sing for you," she said to Kany, "for you who long for someone; may my song bring you closer."

Kany could not speak a word; her lips moved, that was all.

As soon as she had set her bags down, Kany ran to the house of Samou. Old Benfa was not at home. Sibiri was sleeping. Mama Téné was in the kitchen; the other wives were washing clothes around the well. They all laughed when Kany told them that she was going on an errand.

Samou was standing in front of his house. He was talking to a friend, a newspaper in his hand. Kany came running and from fifty yards away, she called out: "Samou, Samou!" Samou threw down the paper and ran to Kany.

Samou! Samou! Kany! Kany! They stood without moving or speaking. Then Samou led her to his house, and there again, there was silence. Never had Kany appeared so shy; everything she wanted to tell Samou escaped her. They both stood, lost in thought, dreaming perhaps of that tomorrow that they would build together.

Samou was now welcome in Old Benfa's family. Mama Téné and Benfa's other wives were already calling him "our son-in-law." Kany's little brothers, Nianson and Karamoko, teased him as was customary. Samou often brought them little gifts. He went out with Kany openly. Sometimes they took a walk towards the hill under the cynical gaze of the baboon, other times they went to the bank of the river to listen to the chants of the boatmen. Kany was happy. Her friends shared in her joy, and Sidi, their leader, said that a new world was beginning.

One day, during a discussion at the house of Sira, he had pompously stated:

"The example of Kany must be followed; no matter how 'sacred' some of our institutions are, we should not hesitate to fight them if they keep us inferior to other people.

"Our parents were right yesterday, but today things have changed. They must understand. Our country's interests demand it."

"Oh no," Samou had answered, "I have thought a lot about what is happening to us. I have been influenced by the older generation who has been to Europe and who has seen many things there. You see, whatever the outcome of this matter, I would never be angry at Kany's parents. They are not the only ones responsible. Our problem is that we were the stake in a contest. We chose the easiest path. We were not brought up with the values of our country. We

96

were impressed and we could not resist. The Europeans destroyed everything in us; yes, indeed, all the values which could have made us carry on as followers of our fathers and as the pioneers of an Africa which, without betraying itself, could assimilate the European teachings. Let us admit it, school has oriented us towards the European world. The result has been that we have wanted to transplant Europe into our villages, into our families. We have not been told anything about our world except that it is backwards."

"Shut up, you don't know what you're talking about," shouted Aliou; and Sira started the phonograph.

One evening, as she was coming back from a walk, Kany saw Famagan and a few of his friends coming out of her house. Sibiri and Old Benfa were with them. Everyone was in a good mood. They were laughing loudly and shaking hands. When they saw Kany, they stopped laughing; there was silence. Kany paused in the hall, her heart pounding. She went to her quarters and started to cry. She understood that it was not over...

The next day, Kany, pretending to have forgotten what she had seen the night before, began to sing the name of Samou in front of the whole family. Old Benfa frowned. His reaction did not go unnoticed by Kany, and it confirmed what she now knew for sure: it was not over.

Indeed, it was not over.

After Old Djigui's message, Old Benfa had said to Famagan:

"I will settle all that with my brother. In the meantime, be patient, I will manage to make Kany see reason."

Old Benfa had prepared his plan of action. Since he could not disobey Old Djigui, who was his older brother, he decided to accept Samou among his family temporarily. Then he could work behind the scenes and take the necessary steps to get the approval of his brother. He would send him a messenger chosen amongst the cleverest minstrels in the city, and Old Djigui, wise among the wise, would again side with the ancients before long. Now, this messenger had left the city the very evening that Kany had come upon Famagan, his friends, Sibiri and Old Benfa.

Thus, since Old Benfa had frowned, Kany had kept quiet. There was a moment of silence; Birama and Nianson looked at each other. The atmosphere grew tense. Birama felt very angry, but dared not say a word and gave his sister a sympathetic look. Old Benfa, as if he were not concerned at all with his entourage, talked of the storm of the previous day and of the likely flooding of the river.

The meal was eaten in silence also. On the men's side, the younger ones sulking at Sibiri and their father had observed an obvious silence. On the women's side, Kany sat sad and quiet. Nothing could cheer her up, neither the teasing of Boubouny, the little pet monkey, nor the little stories of her father's wives. Mama Téné was watching her, sending her furtive glances and trying to arouse her interest in their conversation, but Kany kept silent.

After the meal, Birama received the visit of Sidi, and he told him what was being plotted in the family. Sidi, a bit distressed, said that it did not make sense to him at all.

"My father thinks he is right," Birama told him. "He will never consent to the marriage of Kany and Samou. The other night, I heard a few words of what he was telling one of his friends:

"'The young folks, just because they can read and write, want to lead us. I have always had trouble with my children who go to school. This time, I am going to show them that I am alive and kicking.'"

"It is not time for revolution now," said Sidi gloomily. "We do not know what to do with the older generation anymore. But you see, Birama, the older people, like Old Man Benfa, who have never known anything besides Africa, are usually sincere when they try to impose the past on us. I know families of so-called 'literate people' that are

98

also full of prejudices. When these people marry off their daughter, it is for purely material reasons. Maybe they are the ones we should oppose."

There was a moment of silence. Sidi passed his hand over his face. Then he sighed and continued:

"I just ran across Kerfa-the-fool. He said very strange things to me when I told him of the impending marriage of Kany and Samou. After his usual cackling laugh, he said to me:

"'I would be very much surprised if Old Benfa agreed to this marriage; I like Samou and Kany very much, but unfortunately, that's the way things are.'

"And why is that?

"'It is an old, old story,' he answered me in a mysterious manner. 'I have spent my time with the older people. You have called me an idiot because I am always with old people, or with people from my village. And yet, the company I keep has taught me many things. The elders see you young people as termites attacking the sacred tree. They know you cannot wait to throw everything overboard, as you yourself like to say, Sidi. And believe me, your entire behavior tends to lend them credence. You have done everything to set them up against you. Each family has become a battlefield where young and old confront each other. You could have compromised with them with a little diplomacy, and you would have found the way to conciliation. But alas, on the street, you do not greet them anymore. When they give you some advice, you more or less make fun of them. 'Whirlwind's dust carries seeds of fever,' that makes you laugh, but then why do they teach you in school to sprinkle the floor of your hut before you sweep? No, Old Benfa will not agree. He believes he is right. He is defending from your attacks what his forefathers left him; maybe you should have discussed with them a little, you should have politely pointed out to them some of their mistakes. They would have been proud of you, the old people. They would have given up many things of their own free will. But without any discussion at all, without the slightest explanation, you cry out to them: everything is bad. You have taken a road that now proves to be a dead-end. Poor Kany, poor Samou. But that's the way it is; it is always the best ones who pay.'

"'You are crazy, you are completely crazy,' I said to him.

"But you see, Birama, in a way, Kerfa is right. Old Benfa, as I told you, is sincere! Well... for Kany and Samou, and for us all, let us hope that everything turns out all right."

In the evening, Kany went to talk to Mama Téné in her quarters. She asked her why Old Benfa had frowned when she had sung Samou's name. Mama Téné did not know. Kany then went to talk to Birama. He did not tell her anything either. All he knew was that something was afoot. The other wives of Benfa did not know anything either. Kany felt at a loss; she had the impression that she was in an unknown world, in the middle of people with whom she had nothing in common. She retired to her hut.

The next day, Mama Téné did not see her at breakfast, and so, she went to get her.

"Well, are you coming to eat?"

"I am not hungry."

"Come now, you are not very smart. Come."

"No!"

There was a moment of silence. Mama Téné, who was standing at the door, went in and leaned against the *tara* on which Kany was lying.

"You are still wondering why your father frowned when you sang Samou's name? All I know is that it is improper to speak of your fiancé in the presence of your parents. Did you stop and think about that at all?" she added as she left.

Perceived as rude

Kany jumped up. "Could that be it? It cannot be," she thought. "After all, why not? Maybe nothing is afoot in spite of all; maybe I simply imagined it. Yes, it is my imagination working overtime. I see my mistake. A girl does not sing of her fiancé in front of her parents. She does not speak of him. Oh! what a fool I am!" Her face brightened for a second. Then all of a sudden, she collapsed on the *tara* and broke down. "No, it is not because I sang Samou's name; something is brewing against me, otherwise what would have been the purpose of Famagan's visit? Of course not. Why were Famagan, my father and Sibiri in such a good mood? Something is brewing!"

She got up anyway and walked to the well; she drew two buckets of water, her little toothpick between her lips. She then washed and went to join Mama Téné and the other wives around the pot of steaming gruel. Not that she was hungry, but she hoped to learn something.

When Kerfa came into Samou's house, all his friends were sitting on the same *tara*, looking more or less stiff and awkward. The room was so silent that Kerfa had been surprised to find people in it. Samou, his elbow on his knee, his chin in his hand, was looking steadfastedly through the little window. Sidi had an open book in his hand, but he was staring at the wall instead.

Although Kerfa was a childhood friend of Samou's, he did not hang around with him as much as the others. His presence at this time of the night, when the muezzin had already called the evening prayer, was rather unusual.

On any other day, such an event would have brought exclamations or comments from Sidi. But the leader hardly reacted and answered like the others in a dull voice to the greeting of the visitor.

Kerfa was the first one to be surprised by this apathy. After the discussion he had had with Sidi on the behavior of the young people towards their elders, after all he had said to Sidi, he was expecting a bit of rough treatment from his friends. But now, Sidi had bigger worries. He had overheard a conversation between Famagan and one of his friends. Famagan, exulting, announced his forthcoming marriage; he declared it was only a matter of days. He had sent word to his family in the nearby town. He swore he was preparing a feast that everyone would remember.

In a panic, Sidi had come to talk to Samou. There was nothing more they could do; Kany was lost to them. Birama, who came in a few moments later, was told of their plight. Samou had no hope left. Terribly ill at ease, Birama sat with his back to his friends. Kany's brother was experiencing some feeling of guilt and was truly ashamed. Classmates would comment on Kany's marriage at the beginning of the school year. Old Benfa would be discussed. They would denounce his lack of understanding, and some would even mention his greed. "He sold his daughter" would be the general conclusion.

Birama could already feel the humiliation. He wondered if he would have the courage to go back to school. He would never be the same again, because he would bear, like a stigma, the brand of the unfortunate action of his father. Some of his schoolmates would even judge him as harshly as they judged Old Benfa. Those would not even try to understand, nor to know how hard Birama had struggled to prevent that marriage. Others who, less unfairly, would believe in his genuine friendship for Samou, would perhaps decide that he did not do everything that this friendship required of him. However he looked at it, Birama dreaded his fate; he could not approve of the unkind remarks that would be made to his father, nor could he tolerate them. He could not side with Old Benfa either, because he disapproved very much of this marriage that he had tried to prevent with all his might.

Sidi also was thinking about the consequences of this marriage, although for him things were a little different. "The dreamer," as they called him, had regarded this ordeal as some kind of a proving ground which should, in the end, consecrate their fighting spirit. He could not imagine defeat, because this trial was a prelude to the great struggle to come that Sidi was going to lead with his group. Defeat would mean despair and the end of all dreams.

As a result, Samou, Birama and Sidi grieved over their unfortunate attempt at freedom. They had known moments of hope and reasons to rejoice, yes indeed, but now the world was inexorably closing up on them.

Their distress was easy to understand. It would not have looked out of proportion in the eyes of anyone used to the region and its customs. Africans, who are known with good reason as the friendliest people in the world, can also be savage and cruel. Now, the marriage of Kany was certainly going to bring out reactions that an outsider could not even begin to imagine.

Since they had tried to undermine some of the principles of the community, Samou and his friends had deliberately ostracized themselves. If this marriage took place, they would become outcasts; their presence in any group would then bring painful silence, irritating whispers or cutting remarks. They would be spared nothing.

Those who had admired their courage and acclaimed their success would now be the most merciless. They had admired them, even if they themselves had kept quiet and were apparently obedient, because they too were feeling the crushing burden of tradition. At every step in their lives, they crashed into the obstacles these old principles represented. The elders seemed to openly strew them in their path. Those fearful people would be as cruel, if not more so, than the elders, for Samou and his friends from now on would bear the weight of their dashed hopes. It must also be said that the attempt of Samou and his friends would have a bearing on the future attitude of the elders of the neighborhood and even of the entire city, with regard to this new generation in which they had always detected a penchant for sacrilege.

Samou and his friends would thus have confirmed everything which had been said about these youths who lacked respect and maturity.

105

On the other hand, if, by their own initiative, the young people had succeeded in preventing this marriage, the elders, always careful and wise, would have understood the need to retreat and yield. The younger generation would have proved that they could be firm and stubborn, and those qualities have always been appreciated among the elders.

"I have something to tell you," Kerfa said in a slow, hesitant voice, "something important, and I beg of you to hear me out.

"Listen... Samou, a few days ago, your mother, Mama Coumba, and I undertook to make a certain move. We did not tell anybody, because we wanted to know what would come out of it. Today, I can talk to you about it, because we believe we have succeeded. Kany knows something of it. She came with us the first days, but she knows nothing of our results."

There was a stir. Samou directed his dejected looks at Kerfa who, head down, hands in his pockets, continued in that quavering voice of his:

"Mama Coumba and I went to see a few older people; it wasn't easy. At first, we went to the wrong people; indeed, the first people we talked to were on Famagan's side. They assured us that they knew that Famagan had taken the wrong course, but they had given him their word, and they would back him up to the bitter end.

"After different approaches, we finally succeeded in winning out a few important older people to our cause, including Old Aladji and Mamari the *griot*.[6] They are going to go and talk to Old Benfa tomorrow. Mamary has already been to see Famagan twice. He went with a whole group of *griots*."

"What have you done? Are you crazy?"

---

6. At the same time historian, poet, musician, counselor, the griot is a very important person in traditional African society.

106

"No, I am not crazy. You are the ones who are crazy."

"No, Kerfa, you should not have done that. You have given Famagan and these elders the chance to make fun of us. You put us on our knees before these old people. We do not want their charity; we will not accept alms from them."

"No, listen to me. I know what you are feeling now, it is pride. But there is no room for pride here. Once again, the older people are not your enemies; they are your elders, your fathers. Have you thought about that? They are the people who brought you into this world and who, in the normal order of things, should be guiding you. They have lived under a given system; this system has its laws, and they have respected these laws. They have not been worse off because of that. Quite the contrary. When they impose a specific path for you to follow, they are thinking of you more than of themselves. The old people are rather unhappy. Imagine a man who, very rich yesterday, finds himself without resources today. He is told that his riches are now worthless. His storehouses are full of millet, and he is told that millet is worthless. He owns some cattle, and he is told that cattle are worthless. And this, without any preparation, with the suddenness of a summer rain; the older people are like this man. Yesterday, everyone still believed in them, believed in what they said, and worshiped their god. Today, we cry from the housetops that none of the things that were dear to them deserve our consideration. The old people are all confused, and you, you have disappointed them, because what they expected of you was a sympathetic understanding and a gradual, enlightened introduction to the system that is being forced upon them. For the time being, they are confused. I ask you: is it humane to drive them to the wall? Is it humane to harass them even in their fragile dreams? All Africa is in turmoil today; we have nothing left, neither love nor God. Believe me, your duty does not lie in this minor struggle.

107

"It lies elsewhere. Sidi, I know that you have always been an advocate of power and violence. Day and night you urge us to imitate the Europeans, to abandon everything if necessary, so as to become powerful industrially. You always told me that with power one could solve all problems. I do not agree with you; I never have. Look, we have had three conquering prophets in the Sudan. They tried to establish Islam by the power of their sword. Indeed they have succeeded in conquering animist regions. People have knelt before their power, but they have been unable to win their hearts, and the religion they tried to introduce has not had the following they expected. These regions, although politically dominated, have remained faithful to their fetishes. It is in our time that Islam is winning over these areas. It is winning them over thanks to the courage and self-sacrifice of those humble marabouts, anonymous apostles, who travel the difficult trails with their knapsack and their book. I am not a Muslim. I chose this example because it somewhat illustrates what I have to say to you. I know that the desire to build up your country lives in all of you, Believe me, you will accomplish nothing by force. To follow the example of modern political systems would be a big mistake on your part. You would do better to adopt the armor of the apostles, because you will encounter many difficulties, even among those to whom you want to bring something. Start by thinking of others instead of yourselves. I was well aware that you would not forgive me for undertaking what I have just told you. But believe me, it is a way that I beg you to follow. I hope that my action will open the way that leads to reconciliation. I do not know yet what Old Benfa will say. I would be surprised if he acceded to our request; but the elders, I am sure, will never forget what we have just done. Whether this attempt is a success or not, it will be just another marriage or step. Nobody will call it sacrilege anymore."

Kerfa left, and the room became silent once again; not a word was spoken. Birama heaved a sigh. He was surprised. He looked as if he were coming out of a trance. He cast a quick glance around him and became meditative again. Sidi, his legs crossed, wiggled his foot nervously. Samou stared at the empty space that Kerfa had occupied; he had been visibly affected by all the things his friend had said. His calm expression was quite different from the sanctimonious air he had before.

After all, what Kerfa had done was not so bad. Besides, he thought, there was Mama Coumba, and even Kany knew what was going on. One could not disagree with Mama Coumba or displease Kany. Anyway, the purpose of this venture was to win over Old Benfa. Then Famagan will not be able to honestly brag about it. Besides, it really does not matter at all. The words of Kerfa remind me of the sentiments in the letter that Tiéman wrote to me. How curious that is.

Sidi stood up, went to the window, drew in a deep breath and exhaled vigorously. After his own inner struggle, he found himself not too angered at this new initiative either. It could lead to the marriage of Samou and Kany. The unity of the group would be saved. Moreover, if friends have something to say, if they talk of giving in, their reproaches will be directed at Kerfa. Anyway, why discuss all that? The older people are not our enemies. They mean well. The enemy is rather among those so-called modern individuals who take advantage of their choice positions to rob their own brothers. Vanity, pride, no!

109

The moon was following her changeless course in the clear sky, and her pale light shone down on the courtyard. The daylight seemed to be extended to the chickens still wandering around the courtyard among the jumble of pots and pans. Beggars were going from door to door repeating the hymns their lips never tire of. In the street, a *griot* surrounded by young admirers was reviving the past with his monotonous but ever stirring chanting. The women selling fruit had set themselves under the *kaïlcedrat* trees, and with their little lamps and their faithful customers they formed small, glowing scenes where the redolent mangoes lent their scent to the fables and the colorful oaths. It was one of those moonlit nights which are so frequent.

In Benfa's home, however, it was an unusual night. It was a night when *Héré, that is, peace and happiness,* seemed to have descended upon the house of Kany. For every home has this experience. That is why the word *Héré* is the heart of the various forms of daily greetings. "*Héré* be with you" is the wish that goes right to the heart. With *Héré*, old quarrels are forgotten; grudges due to old quarrels are forgotten too. Warmed by a miraculous breath, hearts open up to friendship. Yesterday's foes become friends, indifference becomes friendliness. Old memories crumble into dust, and the whole family is reborn to a new life, pure and clean as early morn. That is the life celebrated by the women grinding millet in the shade of the

Héré

110

mango tree, when the sun in the zenith rains its fire on backs dripping with sweat. That is the life the Fulani shepherd sings with his one-stringed *kirine* on the burned out trails in the bush; it is a life without hatred, a life of peace and friendship.

During the day, several times, *Gnamatou*, the bird of the travelers, had perched on the little mango tree in the courtyard. Mama Téné and the other wives had wondered what it could mean. *Gnamatou* always foretells the return of an absent friend we long to see. He is the bird of the road. Now we can tell what he wanted to announce to Mama Téné and her companions. It concerned the return of *Héré*, happiness, the peace which had left the Benfa family right at the beginning of the problem of Kany.

Peace had come back that evening. Boubouny, the little monkey, had come close to him, and twice the patriarch was seen patting the little monkey on the head. Never had Boubouny seemed so well behaved. He had not touched the prayer beads left on the sheepskin, or the pots and pans of Mama Téné. Wisdom seemed to have taken possession of him.

Birama had not retired to his room as he usually did. Seated near his father, he was reading by the faint light of the oil lamp. Sibiri was there too, in a lounge chair; time and again, he patted the sheep chewing the cud by his feet. Under the little mango tree, Kany, Mama Téné and the other wives were talking and laughing loudly as usual. It was a night of peace. Differences seemed forgotten, troubles had vanished; bitterness was dead, yes indeed, because here the heart always ruled over words and deeds.

Two figures entered the hall, then two more. The visitors could be identified by the sound of their scuffing slippers: they were the senior elders.

Old Benfa sat up, and Birama closed his book. Sibiri sat up straight while Mama Téné went to get the big mats for guests.

"May the night be kind to you!" called out one of the visitors.

"Peace be with you always," responded Old Benfa.

"Benfa, we greet you."

"Peace be with you."

"Please sit down, Mamari, Aladji, Koniba and Siré."

"Benfa, only one being never makes mistakes; it is the one who never acts."

"True, Mamari."

"Benfa, may God who made heaven and earth accept our prayers."

"True, Mamari."

There was a solemn moment of silence. Old Benfa cleared his throat, but he did not say anything.

"Benfa," Mamari went on, "my father stood by your father's side all his life; he beheld him and admired him among the hunters of wild beasts; between you and me, refusal is not possible."

"True!" whispered Old Benfa.

"Now, Aladji, it is your turn to speak," said Mamari to his neighbor, who nodded as he stroked his beard.

"Benfa," Old Aladji said, "we have come not to right a wrong that you committed but rather so that you may help us not commit one. You know as well as I do that times have changed. You know that, Benfa. To want to act as we did not long ago, and as our fathers did, that would indicate that you did not see all the changes there have been. If we are here, it is not to judge you, as some do, from appearances and thereby commit an error. Benfa, marriage today is not the same as we used to know it.

"In our day, man only spoke sincere words; today, we are confronted with people who devote their skills to feeding their fellow man with false promises.

"In our day, in war as in life, we fought face to face. Today, the strongest one is the one who can best conceal things. Benfa, things have changed. Our children do not

112

want to follow us anymore. They refuse everything we give them. They believe they'll find somewhere else what can only be found at home. What is to be done? Must we make enemies of our children? No! I do not think so. Sooner or later life will teach them the truth. For 'When you are too warm in your hut, you can always make an opening in the wall, but when you are too warm in your neighbor's hut, all you can do is go and sleep under a tree' and 'A home is wonderful only when everyone is willing to do his share of the work.'

"Believe me, Benfa, rather than make these youngsters our adversaries, let us help them. They are unhappy. Their way, they will find it after having walked paths strewn with thorns, but they will find it, because 'From the roots to the leaves, sap rises and never stops.'"

There was a moment of silence; the oil lamp reflected a faint light on the now somber face of Old Aladji.

Old Benfa cleared his throat.

"Aladji, what you have just said is true. We are in a world that we do not know. Today, there is nothing left: no more bonds between father and son, no more honesty between friends, no more respect between young and old. However, in spite of it all, I did not expect that from Kany... I am stubborn because I had given my word to Famagan. Today, it is the only thing that troubles me. When you give your word, Aladji..."

"That's it!" exclaimed Mamari. "I thought of it because I know your honesty; however, set your mind at ease on that score. I have seen Famagan on three separate occasions. I explained to him that this fight does not honor him. He told me he would withdraw if you agree... I also know that you sent a message to your brother Djigui; with your permission, I will go to see him tomorrow."

Old Benfa seemed lost in thought. He raised his eyes to the stars and then looked towards the women, who were now quiet.

Famagan had called the deal off. So Old Benfa had nothing to reproach himself. And then, Aladji and all these elders were as much involved as he was. This did not concern Kany and Birama alone, but all the young people who thought they knew more than their elders. Some day, they would see their mistake. Then they would come back to the elders' world, ready to devote themselves to it, body and soul. When that day would come, they would understand their elders, and all their actions would seem clear, admirable, and wonderful. Their children, to whom they would tell their experiences, would be raised with a new wisdom.

Sibiri made a move and reached out to the water glass with his hand.

"It's empty," Birama said. "I'll get you some."

Old Benfa looked at Birama, who had sprung up and taken the glass. He looked him over from head to toe, standing there in his European clothes. He smiled.

"And you too, my son, some day you will be thirsty."

About the Book

Born in Mali (then French Sudan) in 1928, **Seydou Badian** was a member of the second generation of African intellectuals that rose to defend the value of their own culture and to take a greater role in their political future. His personal involvement in government began in 1957, when he served as French Sudan's minister of rural economy and planning. After the establishment of the Republic of Mali in 1960, he was leader of the radical Marxist group in the government of Modibo Keita. He spent ten years in prison after Keita's 1968 overthrow.

Marie-Thérèse Noiset is associate professor of French at the University of North Carolina at Charlotte.

#17: (Make up your own question about Caught in the Storm)

#16: Defend the village custom of the fathers' choosing husbands for their daughters.

#15: Describe, like an anthropologist, the ideas, customs, values that organize traditional village life

#14: Why is school the ENEMY of the family? pg-9